RANCHO CUCAMONGA
PUBLIC LIBRARY

A NOVELIZATION

A NOVELIZATION

Adapted by Rico Green

Based on *Descendants*, written by

Josann McGibbon & Sara Parriott

Los Angeles • New York

Printed in the United States of America
First Hardcover Edition, July 2015
3 5 7 9 10 8 6 4 2
FAC-020093-15176

Library of Congress Control Number: 2014959690
ISBN 978-1-4847-2614-3

For more Disney Press fun, visit www.disneybooks.com
Visit DisneyDescendants.com

THIS LABEL APPLIES TO TEXT STOCK

To Mom, for lending me her spell book

CHAPTER ONE

I'm Mal, daughter of the evil sorceress Maleficent.
I know what you must be thinking: I'm an
evil villain, too. I mean, how could I *not* be with
a mom like that? She has horns, for badness' sake.
Plus, she cursed Sleeping Beauty and her kingdom all
those years ago. Even all the baddies here on the Isle
of the Lost quake at the sight of her. And this place
brims with all the most evil villains, sidekicks, and
stepmothers and stepsisters ever—basically all the
interesting people.

Twenty years ago, when the Beast finally put
a ring on it and married Belle, he united all the
kingdoms and became king of the good ol' USA—
United States of Auradon (Blech!). He rounded up all

the baddies and booted them off to the Isle of the Lost with a magical barrier to keep us here. This isle is my 'hood. No magic. No Wi-Fi. No way out for me and my wicked friends.

But then this happened. . . .

CHAPTER TWO

MEET BEN. SON OF THE BEAST AND BELLE. PRETTY EYES, KILLER MANE. YOU CAN SEE THE RESEMBLANCE. ANYWAY, BEN STARTED THE WHOLE THING WITH HIS BIG IDEA ONE DAY. . . .

In the castle of Beauty and the Beast, their son, Ben, kept gazing out the window.

Even from way across the sparkling blue sea, Ben could see the magical barrier flickering and shimmering over the Isle of the Lost. It was so pretty, that far-off isle of exiled prisoners . . . but Ben couldn't help feeling sad at the sight of it.

The royal tailor was fitting Ben into his blue coronation suit, jotting Ben's measurements down on a notepad, when Belle and Beast strolled into the room.

"How is it possible that you're going to be crowned king next month?" Beast said, blinking his blue eyes behind black bold-frame glasses. The gold crown atop his head glittered. Soon it would be passed on to Ben. "You're just a baby," he said.

"He's turning sixteen, dear," said Belle, looking lovely in her yellow dress.

"Hey, Pops," said Ben.

"*Sixteen?*" said Beast, taking off his glasses. "That's far too young to be crowned king. I didn't make a good decision until I was at least . . . forty-two." He smiled and tucked his glasses into his jacket pocket.

Belle faced him. "Uh, you decided to marry me at twenty-eight," she said.

"It was either you or a teapot," said Beast as he winked at Ben.

Ben chuckled.

"Kidding," said Beast, his eyebrows dancing.

"Mom, Dad, I've chosen my first official proclamation!" said Ben.

Beast and Belle looked at each other and smiled.

"I've decided that the children on the Isle of the Lost should be given a chance . . . to live here in Auradon," said Ben.

His parents gawked at him, wide-eyed.

The tailor, sensing the sudden tension, sat down.

"Every time I look out at the island," Ben said, gesturing toward the isle out the window, "I feel like they've been abandoned."

"The children of our *sworn* enemies?" said Beast. *"Living among us?"*

"We start out with a few at first—only ones who need our help the most," said Ben. "I've already chosen them."

"Have you?" said Beast, his eyebrows furrowing.

Belle placed a hand on Beast's arm. "I gave *you* a second chance," she said. She looked at Ben. "Who are their parents?"

"Cruella De Vil, Jafar, Evil Queen . . ." Ben took a breath. "And Maleficent."

The tailor gasped and dropped his notepad.

"Maleficent?" shouted Beast. "She is the worst villain in the land!"

"Dad, just hear me out here!" said Ben.

"I won't hear of it!" said Beast, shaking his finger. "They are guilty of *unspeakable* crimes!"

Butlers opened the door and the tailor slunk quietly out of the room.

"But their children are innocent," said Ben. "Don't you think they deserve a shot at a normal life?"

Beast stared long and hard at his son.

"Dad," said Ben, giving him a pleading look.

Beast looked at Belle and said, "I suppose the children *are* innocent."

HA!
AND THERE IT IS.
SUCKERS!

CHAPTER THREE

$\int$ OME KIDS GROW UP HEARING LAME LULLABIES AND STUPID FLOWERY FAIRY TALES.

BUT ON THIS ISLAND, IT'S ALWAYS BEEN ABOUT "LONG LIVE EVIL."

On the Isle of the Lost, Mal spray-painted a battered city wall.

With her purple hair, leather jacket with a decal of two dragons on the back, and tough-as-nails boots, Mal had trouble written all over her—which was precisely what she was going for. The bilious green spray paint spelled out LONG LIVE EVIL. Mal holstered her paint can, reveled in her work, and stepped into the bustling marketplace, where she was quickly swept up in the throng and blended into the sea of haggard, worn faces.

Jay, son of Jafar, watched Mal vanish into the crowd as he looked out over the bazaar from the rooftop of a nearby building. Oozing confidence, he had long dark hair and biceps that bulged out of his leather vest. He smiled. His eyes glinted dangerously. In several cobra-like moves, Jay leaped and slid down a rusty ladder from the rooftop. Those who knew of Jay would say that he was dirty, no good, bad to the bone.

Evie, daughter of Evil Queen, spotted Jay making his way toward the street and returned to strutting across a table, where disheveled urchins were trying to eat. They ogled Evie's dazzling smile, dark wavy hair, and hypnotizing eyes. She wore all blue, with a necklace that had a red gem topped by a gold crown. She carried a red box-shaped purse. She was a natural beauty, but it was hard to tell under all the makeup. Her mom had taught her that looks were everything. She glanced around to see Jay was gone.

Carlos, son of Cruella De Vil, spied Evie as he climbed out of a window and stepped into the rowdy street. Carlos was a skinny teen with white hair with black roots, and he was all decked out in a red, white, and black leather jacket and boots. As he walked through the bazaar, he stole a handkerchief and then swiped an apple. Villagers considered him a callous lowlife. And he loved them for it.

Evie and Mal emerged from a back alley. Carlos raced up to them as Jay leaped down from a building to join them. The four friends were united once again. They slid aside a chain-link gate and marched from warehouse to warehouse. They ran through clothes hanging on lines and banged old washing basins. Mal spray-painted an *M* onto a shower curtain. Jay stole a teapot. Evie flirted with a merchant. Carlos kicked over a food basket. As they stomped out onto the filthy street, the friends struck fear and respect into the hearts of the street hawkers, pickpockets, and scam artists. The four teens were truly rotten to the core.

Mal snatched a lollipop out of a child's hand, and it began to cry. She held up the lollipop triumphantly. Mal's friends laughed. They were pleased with her stunt.

Suddenly, a shadow loomed in their path, and all the merchants scampered away, hiding in shops. It could only mean one thing.

Henchmen appeared and cleared the way to make room for Her Royal Wickedness, Maleficent, Mistress of Evil. Her horns were wrapped in leather and she carried a scepter, her eyes flashing green.

"Hi, Mom," said Mal with a mischievous smile.

"Stealing candy, Mal?" said Maleficent. "I'm *so* disappointed."

Mal scrunched up her face. "It was from a *baby*," she said cheerily, holding out the lollipop. Mal's friends laughed again at just how very mean she could be.

Maleficent smiled. "That's my nasty little girl!" She snatched the lollipop from Mal's hand, spit on it, clamped it in her armpit, and handed it to one of her henchmen. "Give it back to the dreadful creature," Maleficent said, eyes gleaming.

"Mom . . ." Mal said, annoyed at how her mom always had to one-up her.

The henchman trotted off to return the lollipop to the mother of the baby.

"It's the deets, Mal, that make the difference between mean and *truly evil*," said Maleficent. She smiled and waved to the grateful mother. She looked back at Mal. "When I was your age, I was cursing entire kingdoms." She gestured grandly.

Mal mouthed along: *"Cursing entire kingdoms!"* She rolled her eyes.

"Walk with me," said Maleficent, putting her hand on her daughter's shoulder and guiding her forward. "See, I'm just trying to teach you the thing that really counts: how to be me."

"I know that," said Mal, nodding, "and I'll do better."

"Oh! There's news," said Maleficent, whipping around. "I buried the lede!" She pointed at Mal and her friends. "You four have been chosen to go to a *different* school. In Auradon."

At these words, Evie, Jay, and Carlos made to bolt, only to be snatched up by Maleficent's henchmen.

Mal gawked at her mom, eyes widening.

Her friends stopped struggling against their captors.

"*What?*" said Mal. "Mom, you have to be joking."

"Nope!" said Maleficent. "You'll be joining the bastion of privilege and exclusivity of . . . Auradon Prep." The words left a sour-apple taste in her mouth.

"Mom! I'm not going to some boarding school filled to the brim with prissy pink princesses!" said Mal.

"And perfect princes!" said Evie dreamily as she stepped beside Mal.

Mal glared at her.

Evie's smile vanished. "Ugh!" she said, feigning a look of disgust.

"I don't do uniforms," said Jay. "Unless it's leather. You feelin' me?" He grinned and tried to high-five a terrified Carlos, who stepped toward Maleficent.

"I read somewhere that they allow dogs in Auradon," Carlos said. "Mom said they're rabid pack animals who eat boys who don't behave." He gulped, unblinking.

Jay snuck up to Carlos and barked in his ear.

Carlos jumped back and Jay laughed.

"Yeah, Mom, we're not going," said Mal matter-of-factly. "You are not going to start to see me doing curtsies and book reports."

"You're thinking small, punkin'," said Maleficent. "It's all about *world domination*!" She licked her lips. Then she turned to her henchmen. "Knuckleheads!" She turned on her heel, sweeping her cloak, and took off down the empty street, flanked by her devoted thugs. "Mal!" she sang over her shoulder, beckoning her daughter forth.

Mal and her friends exchanged glances and followed Maleficent.

CHAPTER FOUR

WORLD DOMINATION? OF COURSE. IT'S ALL MOM EVER TALKS ABOUT.

THAT . . . AND REVENGE. TYPICAL EVIL OLD MOM. WELL, HERE WE GO!

Maleficent's tenement apartment sat directly above Bargain Castle.

It was dark, dusty, and dirty—just to Maleficent's liking. The colored windowpanes were mismatched and blocked out the sun. Lights in green crystals swayed from the high ceiling. The whole foul place smelled of sulfur. Maleficent, filing her nails, was seated in her tall green throne chair with her feet propped up. Mal and her three friends and their three parents sat around the apartment, waiting for

Maleficent to explain why she had summoned all of them.

The villains had seen better days. Cruella, with her wild black-and-white hair, wore a ratty, nearly bald black-and-white dog-fur coat, which sported a bejeweled stuffed toy Dalmatian head next to her neck. She stroked it lovingly as if it were alive. Jafar, with his trademark mustache and goatee, was rocking a potbelly, a comb-over, and puffy Sansabelt pants. Evil Queen, a former beauty, pulled at her cosmetically altered face and stared into a mirror. Mal, Evie, Jay, and Carlos feared their parents nonetheless.

"You will go," Maleficent commanded the teens. "You will find the Fairy Godmother and you will bring me back her magic wand." She blew on her nails. "Easy peasy."

"What's in it for us?" asked Mal.

"Matching thrones," said Maleficent. "Hers and hers crowns."

Carlos gestured to his friends. "Um, I—I think she meant *us*."

Ignoring him, Maleficent tossed her nail file

over her shoulder, stood, and beckoned Mal to her. "It's all about you and me, baby," she said, leaning in close to Mal. "Do you enjoy watching innocent people suffer?"

"Well, yeah! I mean, who doesn't?" said Mal.

"Well, then get me that wand! And you and I can see all that and so much more!" said Maleficent. "And with that wand and my scepter"—she held up her arms—"*I will be able to bend both good and evil to my will!*"

Evil Queen lowered her mirror. "*Our* will," she said.

Cruella pointed at Evil Queen and nodded.

"*Our* will, *our* will," Maleficent said, trying to save face. She looked at Mal. "And if you refuse, you're grounded for the rest of your life, missy," she said firmly.

"*What?*" cried Mal, distressed. "Mom!"

Maleficent stared into her daughter's eyes. Mal stared right back at her. The stare intensified. It was a test of power and focus. Mal and her mom did this every so often. Maleficent always won. Mal tore away her gaze. "Fine, whatever," Mal said.

"I won," said Maleficent.

"Malef, relax," said Evil Queen. "You're going to pop a vein and that is a look no one can rock."

Cruella cackled.

"Did her face just move?" Maleficent asked Cruella, pointing at Evil Queen.

Cruella used her thumb and forefinger to indicate "a little bit."

"Someone alert the media!" said Maleficent.

"Hilarious," said Evil Queen sarcastically. "Evie! My little Evil-ette in training."

Evie ran over and sat obediently across the table from her mother.

"You just find yourself a prince with a big castle and a mother-in-law wing," said Evil Queen.

"And lots and lots of mirrors," said Evie and her mom in unison.

Evie beamed and clasped her hands.

"No laughing," her mother told her. "Wrinkles."

Evie's smile vanished and she pouted.

Maleficent looked at them and sighed.

"Well, they're not taking my Carlos," said

Cruella, caressing her son's head. "I'd miss him too much."

"Really, Mom?" asked Carlos.

"Yes!" Cruella said. "Who would touch up my roots? Fluff my fur and scrape my bunions off my feet?" She kicked up a leg and Carlos caught her foot in his hand.

He looked miserable. "Maybe a new school wouldn't be the worst thing. . . ."

"Carlos, they have dogs in Auradon!" said Cruella, stroking his cheek.

Carlos looked petrified and shook his head. "Oh, no! I'm not going!"

"Ugh," said Maleficent.

"Jay's not going, either!" said Jafar. "I need him to stock the shelves in my store." He looked at his son. "What did you score?" he asked him.

Jay laughed and pulled a variety of stolen trinkets—one of the last items being an old lamp—from his vest, sleeve cuffs, and boots and handed them over to Jafar.

"A lamp!" Jafar grabbed it and rubbed it furiously.

"Dad, I already tried," said Jay, shaking his head.

"Well, Evie's not going anywhere until we get rid of this unibrow." Evil Queen eyed Evie, extracted a pair of tweezers, and approached her daughter's eyebrows.

"Will it hurt?" asked Evie.

"Beauty is pain, darling, beauty is pain," said Evil Queen as she plucked.

Maleficent addressed the room. "Am I here? Was I speaking? What is *wrong* with you all? People used to cower at the mention of our names! For twenty years, *I* have searched for a way off this island."

Evie began to pluck her mother's eyebrows.

"Ouch!" said Evil Queen.

"For twenty years," continued Maleficent, "they have robbed us of our *revenge*."

"Ouch!" said Evil Queen as Evie kept plucking.

"Revenge on Snow White and her horrible little men," Maleficent told Evil Queen.

"Ouch . . ." said Evil Queen at Maleficent's words.

Maleficent turned to Jafar. "Revenge on Aladdin and his bloated Genie!"

Jafar shook his fists.

Maleficent rounded on Cruella. "Revenge on every squeaky Dalmatian that escaped *your* clutches."

"Oh, but they didn't get Baby," said Cruella, stroking the stuffed toy dog head on her vest. "They didn't get the . . ." She wheezed maniacally. "They didn't get the Baby!"

Jafar locked eyes with Maleficent. "I am with you!"

Maleficent returned the stare. "Who *are* you?" she asked him.

"Jafar? The grand tsar of Agrabah?" he said.

"And I, *Maleficent*, the most evilest of them all . . ." she said. "I will finally have my revenge on Sleeping Beauty and her relentless prince." She turned to her friends. "Villains! Our day has come." She turned to Evil Queen and nodded at Evie. "E.Q., give her the magic mirror."

Evil Queen studied her brows in the shards of glass that used to be her magic mirror. "One minute, *s'il vous plaît*," said Evil Queen, angling her face and studying her reflection.

"Now!" said Maleficent.

"Oh, for badness' sake!" said Evil Queen. "World domination can wait another thirty seconds!" She handed her mirror to Evie.

"*This* is your magic mirror?" asked Evie, sounding disappointed.

"Well," said Evil Queen, "it ain't what it used to be. Then again, neither are we!" She gestured to Maleficent, Cruella, and Jafar, and they laughed. "It will help you find things."

Evie's face lit up. "Like a prince!" she said.

"Like my waistline," said Evil Queen.

"*Like the magic wand!* Hello!" said Maleficent. She looked thoughtful. "I need my book. My spell book. Ah! The safe!" She tried to open the old refrigerator in her kitchen. "I can't open it," she said. "Someone help me! I need to get in! It's broken! I can't get in!"

Everyone looked on as she banged the refrigerator until, finally, Evil Queen pulled its handle and the door opened. Maleficent reached in and retrieved the book.

"Ah! My spell book!" she said. "Come, come, darling," she said to Mal. She lovingly stroked the book's brown leathery cover, which featured a gold embossed dragon. "There she is! It doesn't work here, but it will in Auradon." She looked at Evil Queen. "Remember when we were spreading evil and ruining lives?" asked Maleficent.

"Like it was yesterday," said Evil Queen.

The two women started to get teary-eyed.

Maleficent spun to Mal. "And now, you will be making your own memories. . . ." She offered the spell book to Mal, but before Mal could take it, she snatched it away. "By doing exactly as I tell you," she said, shoving the spell book into Mal's arms.

"Door," Maleficent said to Evil Queen, gesturing to the door.

A horn sounded from the street.

"Let's get this party started!" said Jay.

"Carlos! Come!" said Cruella.

Evie checked herself out in her mirror.

"Who is the fairest of them all?" Evil Queen asked her.

"Me," said Evie.

"Ugh!" said Evil Queen.

"You," said Evie.

"Yes!" said Evil Queen. "Let's go."

Jafar pulled Jay aside for a private exchange. "Now recite our mantra."

"There's no team in 'I,'" said Jay.

Jafar smiled. "Run along. You're making me tear up!"

As everyone filed out of the room, Maleficent threw open the doors and led Mal onto the balcony. They looked over the busy isle streets strung with lights and gazed across the sea. Auradon Prep could be seen nestled in the majestic green mountains. Mal couldn't believe that she'd be there, and so soon.

"The future of the free world rests on your shoulders," said Maleficent. She set a hand on Mal's shoulder. "Don't blow it." She winked and disappeared inside.

Mal lingered on the balcony, not taking her eyes off Auradon. She was afraid but also excited. She wondered if there was someone on the isle looking back at her.

"Mal!" her mother sang, beckoning her.

Mal headed back inside, but not before giving the tiny dot that was Auradon Prep one last look.

From below, the horn honked again, a reminder that it was time to depart.

CHAPTER FIVE

THE FUTURE OF THE FREE WORLD? DON'T BLOW IT?
Jeez. Talk about no pressure. Away we go!

A black stretch limo was parked outside Maleficent's tenement.

It looked wildly out of place in the squalid city. Villagers crowded around it curiously. Jay, Carlos, and Evie walked outside, whooping with glee to see their ride.

"Ugh," said Evil Queen, eying the villagers. "Smells like common folk."

The driver emerged from the limo in a crisp gray suit and dark sunglasses. He took the teens' luggage—Jay's carpetbag, Evie's suitcase and sewing machine, and Carlos's big black trash bag—and loaded it into the trunk. Jay swiped the crown-shaped hood ornament and climbed into the limo along with Evie and Carlos. Mal handed the driver her bag, and he tossed it in and slammed the trunk shut. She took one last look up at the balcony, where her mom gave her an "I have my eye on you" sign. Mal nodded.

She hopped into the limo.

The driver slid into his seat and shut the door. "The jackals have landed," he said into a mike inside his lapel.

The villains waved good-bye to their children from outside the limo as it began to roll. On the street, the villagers looked on as the limo cruised away.

Mal and her friends took in the inside of the limo. They ogled all the buttons, gadgets, colored lights, refreshments, and vast arrays of chocolates, gumballs, jawbreakers, jelly beans, rock candies, and other sweets. Jay wrenched open the fridge. His friends played with the sound system, unwrapped candies and opened cans of soda, and pressed every button, quickly trashing the limo.

Evie went at Mal with a makeup brush. "You're looking a little washed out."

"Ew, stop," said Mal, batting her away. "I'm plotting."

"Well, it's not very attractive," said Evie, gnawing on blue rock candy.

Carlos wolfed down a chocolate peanut butter cup and shook his head with wonder. "Oh! These! It's salty like nuts but it's sweet like I don't know what."

"Let me see," said Jay.

Carlos opened his mouth for Jay to look at the chewed-up peanut butter cup on his tongue. Some fell out. Jay took a cup from Carlos and popped it into his mouth.

Mal clicked a remote. The screen that separated the teens from the driver opened.

"Look!" said Evie, now that she had a clear view out the front of the limo.

The four teens stared ahead at the ruined remains of a bridge and the impenetrable barrier. There was just sea ahead. It looked like they were going to be driven straight into the water. They cowered.

"It's a trap!" said Carlos, terrified.

They all screamed. Carlos jumped onto Jay, and Evie clung to Mal for dear life. The driver pushed a remote attached to the visor. The limo hit the ruins of the bridge and barreled through the barricade. They did not hurtle into the sea. Instead, a magnificent bridge appeared under the steady wheels of the limo. Quickly, Mal and her friends composed themselves, embarrassed about losing their cool. Jay peeled Carlos off him.

"What just happened?" asked Carlos.

"It must be magic!" said Evie.

Mal tapped the wall behind the driver. "Hey!" She held up the remote she had in her hand. "Did this little button just open up the magic barrier?" she asked him.

"Nope." The driver indicated the remote on his visor. "*This* one opens the magic barrier." He motioned at the remote Mal held. "That one opens my garage. And this one . . ." He pushed a button and the screen slid up, shutting off Mal and her friends.

"Nasty. I like that guy," said Mal, smiling.

The limo traveled across the bridge, which continued to extend over the wide expanse of water toward Auradon. The bridge behind the limo disappeared, leaving no way for them to travel back or for anyone to follow. The driver pulled the limo into the sunny kingdom of Auradon and slowed in front of a sign that made Mal and her friends gag:

WELCOME TO AURADON PREP.
GOODNESS DOESN'T GET ANY BETTER.

CHAPTER SIX

ELCOME TO AURADON PREP. HOME OF THE AURADON FIGHTING KNIGHTS. . . .

HOW *CUTE*—YEAH, SO I THINK I'M OFFICIALLY GOING TO BE SICK.

The limo cruised through the sprawling green campus and came to a stop. An impressive building with a flower garden loomed before them. A group of curious students in blue-and-gold uniforms waited outside the limo, waving welcome flags. A marching band started to play with great gusto. The driver opened the limo door, and Mal, Evie, Jay, and Carlos tumbled out. They were about as undignified as it got.

Jay was yanking at a scarf that Carlos was clutching.

"You got everything else, why do you want this?" Carlos asked.

"'Cause *you* want it!" said Jay, wrestling Carlos to the ground and pinning him there with his foot. In their squabble, they didn't notice the group of students watching them. The students backed away at the sight of them fighting, and the band dribbled to a wheezing stop.

A smiling woman stepped through a clump of students with her arms outstretched as if she were about to hug someone. She had brown hair pulled back in a loose bun, pearl earrings, and a lavender dress with a pink bow at the neck.

Mal noticed the woman and alerted her friends. "Guys, guys, guys," Mal said from the side of her mouth. *"We have an audience."* Then she put on a fake smile and struck a fetching pose. Evie quickly followed suit, resting her hands on her hips.

Jay smiled and told his audience, "Just *cleaning up*." He helped Carlos to his feet.

The woman addressed Jay. "Leave it like you found it!" She grinned. "And by that, I mean just leave it." She gave Jay a pointed look.

Jay tossed all his loot back into the limo.

The woman smiled and nodded.

Then Jay noticed a pretty student with caramel-colored skin and chocolate-brown hair. She wore a blue sweater, a pink dress, and a gleaming gold necklace. He sauntered up to her with a smile and said, "Hello, foxy. The name's Jay."

The girl laughed, then stopped.

The woman leaned in between Jay and the student. "Welcome to Auradon Prep," she said.

Jay's smile faded.

"I'm Fairy Godmother. Headmistress." She bowed elegantly.

"*The* Fairy Godmother?" asked Mal.

Fairy Godmother nodded.

"As in 'Bibbidi-Bobbidi-Boo'?" asked Mal, pretending to wave a wand.

"Bibbidi-Bobbidi-you-know-it!" said Fairy Godmother.

Mal gave her a forced good-girl smile. "Yeah, I always wondered what it felt like for Cinderella when you just . . . appeared out of nowhere! With that sparkling *wand* and warm smile . . . and that sparkling *wand*." She flashed a big cheesy smile.

Carlos licked chocolate off his fingers as Mal spoke.

"That was a long time ago," said Fairy God-mother. "And as I always say, don't focus on the past or you'll miss the future!" She smiled. "*Wherever* you wind up!"

"It's so good to finally meet you all," said a hand-some young man as he stepped forward and clasped his hands. He wore a navy suit jacket that sported the Auradon Prep crest, a hankie in the breast pocket, and a pastel plaid tie. "I'm Ben."

"*Prince* Benjamin," said the girl beside him. "Soon to be king!" she squealed.

"You had me at 'prince,'" Evie said as she stepped forward and stared into Ben's eyes. "My mom's a queen, which makes me a princess." She started to bow.

"The Evil Queen has no royal status here," said the girl, "and neither do you."

Ben gave the girl a look that said "cool it." "This is Audrey . . ." he said.

"*Princess* Audrey," said Audrey, taking Ben's hand. "His *girlfriend*. Right, Bennyboo?" She flashed a smile at Ben and tucked her chin.

Ben let out a short laugh.

"Ben and Audrey are going to show you all around," Fairy Godmother told Mal and her friends, "and I'll see you all tomorrow. 'The doors of wisdom *are never shut*!' But the library hours are from eight to eleven, and as you may have heard, I have a little thing about curfews." She smiled, turned away from Mal and her friends, and walked toward a building, with the marching band following in her footsteps.

Ben smiled and approached Mal and her friends. "It is so, so, *so* good to finally meet you all." Jay punched him playfully. Ben shook hands with Mal, Carlos, and Evie, looking into Mal's eyes with a great searing intensity. "This is a momentous occasion," he said, "and one I hope will go down in history as the day our two peoples began to heal." Evie held his hand for too long. Audrey pulled Ben away.

Mal, imitating Ben's tone, said, "Or the day that you showed four peoples where the bathrooms are."

Mal's friends laughed.

Ben grinned. "A little bit over the top?"

"A little more than a little bit," said Mal.

"Well, so much for my first impression," said Ben. He laughed.

Mal laughed, too. She stared at him for a moment, before looking away.

Audrey glared at her through a smile. "Hey! You're Maleficent's daughter, aren't you?" Then she said in a disingenuous voice, "I totally don't blame you for your mother trying to kill my parents and stuff. Oh, my mom's Aurora. Sleeping—"

"Beauty. Yeah, I've heard the name," said Mal, cutting her off. "You know, and I totally don't blame your grandparents for inviting *everyone in the world* except for my mother to their stupid christening."

Audrey blasted a fake smile. "Water under the bridge!"

"Totes!" said Mal, putting on an even bigger fake smile.

Both girls fake laughed and let the laughter fizzle out in unison.

Ben clapped his hands together. "Okay! So how about a tour?" he said happily. He headed toward the garden, sharing facts about the school and its history.

The teens looked up into the face of a fearsome statue that resembled Ben's father in Beast form. Ben clapped and it came to life and growled. Carlos squealed and jumped into Jay's arms. Ben, noticing Carlos's fear, gave a quick double clap. The statue magically transformed into the Beast as a young prince. Carlos relaxed a little.

"Carlos, it's okay. My father wanted his statue to morph from beast to man to remind us that anything is possible," said Ben.

"Does he shed much?" asked Mal.

"Yeah, Mom won't let him on the couch," said Ben with a serious expression.

Mal and he exchanged looks. Mal gave a wry smile and he smiled back.

Ben continued his tour. Jay put Carlos down. Carlos clapped to get the statue to come alive again. Nothing happened. He raced ahead to catch up with the group.

Inside the building, there was a fireplace, dark wood staircases, chandeliers, and stained glass windows that made the place feel warm and sunny.

"So, you guys have a lot of magic here in Auradon?" Mal asked. "Like wands and things like that?"

"Yeah, it exists, of course, but it's pretty much retired," said Ben. "Most of us here are just ordinary mortals."

"Who happen to be kings and queens," added Mal.

"That's true!" said Audrey snootily, draping Ben's arm over her shoulder. "Our royal blood goes back hundreds of years." She looked at Ben possessively.

Ben took his arm off her. "Doug!" he said when he noticed a nerdy boy with thick glasses heading down the stairs. The boy was wearing a blue-and-gold marching band uniform and carried a clipboard. "Doug! Doug, come down!" Ben clapped a hand on

Doug's shoulder. "This is Doug," he announced. "He's going to help you with your class schedules and show you the rest of the dorms." He looked right at Mal. "I'll see you later, okay? And if you need anything at all, feel free to—"

"*Ask Doug,*" blurted out Audrey. She fake laughed and dragged Ben away.

"Hi, guys," said Doug. "I'm Dopey's son? As in"—he started counting on his fingers—"Dopey, Doc, Bashful, Happy, Grumpy, Sleepy, and . . ." Evie caught Doug's eye. "*Heigh-ho,*" he said to her, completely charmed.

Evie went nose to nose with him. "Evie. Evil Queen's daughter." She started to twirl her hair flirtatiously.

"So, about your classes," said Doug. "I put in the requirements already. History of Woodsmen and Pirates, Safety Rules for the Internet, and"—he cleared his throat—"Remedial Goodness 101."

"Let me guess . . ." said Mal. She popped a piece of candy into her mouth. "New class?"

Doug nodded sheepishly.

"Come on, guys," Mal said, dropping the

wrapper on the floor. "Let's go find our dorms." She started up a flight of stairs. Carlos, Jay, and Evie followed her.

"Oh! Uh, yeah, your dorms are that way, guys," said Doug, pointing in the opposite direction.

As Mal and her friends came back down the stairs and headed in the direction he indicated, Doug hung back, counting through the dwarves again. "Dopey, Doc, Bashful, Happy, Grumpy, Sleepy, and . . ."

"Sneezy," said Carlos, passing him and ascending the opposite staircase.

Doug sighed and looked at the ceiling.

Upstairs, Mal and Evie opened the door to their dorm room. It was light and airy and dappled in sunlight. The white canopy beds were covered with pink pillows, and flowery curtains fluttered gently in the fresh breeze from the open windows.

Evie's eyes widened with delight as Mal's narrowed in horror.

"Wow," said Evie. "This place is so amazing—"

"Gross," said Mal.

"I know, right?" said Evie, changing her tune.

"Amazingly *gross*. Ew!" When Mal wasn't looking, Evie couldn't help giving a silent gasp of joy at her new crib.

"I am going to need some serious sunscreen," said Mal, arms crossed.

"Yeah," said Evie.

"E," said Mal, pointing to the windows. She closed the curtains as Evie moved to other windows in the room and did the same, plunging the dorm into darkness.

"Whoa!" said Mal. "That is much better."

CHAPTER SEVEN

I T'S TIME TO MAKE A PLAN TO STEAL THE WAND.
THE SOONER WE GET OUT OF HERE, THE BETTER.

That night, Mal and Evie set out for Jay and Carlos's room to plot the wand heist.

With its wide-screen TV and wood-paneled walls, dark plaid curtains, and high ceiling, Jay and Carlos's room was a sumptuous blend of old money and state-of-the-art technology, which typified Auradon. Carlos faced the wide-screen TV, playing a fun simulation video game with nunchakus while Mal and Evie walked over to Jay.

Jay pulled French fries from his pocket.

"Jay," Mal said. "What are you doing?"

"It's called stealing," Jay said, tossing the fries onto his bed to join the assortment of other items he'd stolen from the school already, which included a few gold rings, tokens, coin purses, a watch, and a half-eaten pizza.

"What's the point?" asked Mal.

"Well, it's like buying whatever I want, except it's free," said Jay, pulling a laptop from his vest.

"Okay. So you could do that. Or you could leave all of this here and pick it up *when we take over the world*," said Mal with a wide smile.

"You sound just like your mom!" Evie told her.

"Thank you!" Mal said to Evie.

"You do it your way and I'll do it mine," said Jay.

"Die, suckers!" Carlos shouted at his virtual foes in the video game. "Jay, come check this thing out!" he said, handing over the nunchakus.

Jay took them and stepped in front of the TV. His biceps bulged as he swung the weapon. Carlos watched him, laughing and whooping as Jay fought off the animated attackers.

"Guys!" said Mal. "Do I have to remind you what we're all here for?"

"Fairy Godmother, blah, blah, blah," said Jay as he swung. "Magic wand, blah, blah, blah."

Evie laughed at him.

"This is our *one* chance to prove ourselves to our parents," said Mal.

Evie stopped laughing and faced Mal.

"To prove that we are evil and vicious and ruthless and cruel," said Mal.

Jay and Carlos stared at her, too. She had their attention.

"Yeah?" Mal asked them.

Her friends nodded solemnly.

"Evie, mirror me," said Mal.

Mal and Evie sat at the table as Jay and Carlos gathered around them.

Evie lifted her mirror. "Mirror, mirror, on the . . . in my hand. Where is Fairy Godmother's wand"—she searched for a rhyming word—"stand?"

In the mirror, there was an extreme close-up of the sparkling wand.

"There it is!" said Evie.

"Zoom out," said Carlos.

"Magic Mirror, not so close," Evie whispered into it.

The mirror showed a map of Earth.

"Closer," said Evie.

The mirror showed the state.

"Closer," she said again.

The mirror showed the town.

"Closer," she said once more.

"Can I go back to my game? I'm on level three," said Carlos.

"Stop!" said Jay.

They peered at the mirror, which showed an old building lit by blue lights, with an engraved sign in front of it that read MUSEUM OF CULTURAL HISTORY.

"It's in a museum," said Mal. "Do we know where that is?"

Carlos typed something on the laptop. "Two point three miles from here," he said, turning it so his friends could see. He went back to playing his video game.

Mal opened the door to the room and checked the hall. The coast was clear.

Jay and Evie followed her down the hall. Jay called Carlos's name over his shoulder, and Carlos stopped playing his game and ran out the door after his friends.

The lawns of the prep school were dark as the gang made its way to the museum. After some walking, they eventually approached an impressive building marked MUSEUM OF CULTURAL HISTORY. It had tall, imposing stone pillars.

"Check your mirror," Mal whispered to Evie.

"Is my mascara smudged?" asked Evie. She checked her eyes in the mirror.

"Yeah. Hey, while you're at it, why don't you see if you can find us *the wand*," said Mal.

"Sure," said Evie. She held out her mirror. "This way!"

They followed Evie around to the back of the building. The group stopped at a set of double doors and peered through their windows. A guard sat at the front desk, spinning in a chair. There were several monitors in front of him. On the monitors were iconic artifacts from all the famous fairy tales: King Beast's mystical rose, Cinderella's glass slipper, the Genie of Agrabah's lamp, King Triton's trident.

The guard spun to face the doors, and Mal and her friends ducked.

When some time had passed, they peeked back

through the windows and studied a small spinning wheel on a pedestal that was a showcased display—Maleficent's spinning wheel.

"*That's* your mother's spinning wheel?" said Carlos. He and Jay laughed.

"Yeah, it's kinda dorky," Jay added.

"It's magic," said Mal defensively. "It doesn't have to *look* scary." Mal flipped open her spell book, found a page, looked through the window at the guard, and began to incant: *"Magic spindle, do not linger. Make my victim prick a finger. . . ."*

Nothing happened to the guard.

"Impressive," said Jay, shaking his head.

"I got chills," said Carlos, mocking her. He and Jay chuckled.

"You know what?" Mal said, annoyed. She concentrated. Her eyes flashed green. *"Prick the finger, prick it deep. Send my enemy off to sleep,"* she said.

The guard stood and started walking toward the spinning wheel as if he was in a trance. He reached out his finger and touched the spindle. Then he yawned, sat down next to the spinning wheel, curled up on his side, and fell right asleep.

Mal let out a laugh. "Not so dorky now," she said smugly. She tried to open the door. It was locked. She yanked a few times.

Jay pushed everyone aside. "Stand back," he said. He backed up, ready to take a leaping kick at the door.

Mal stared at the door and said, *"Make it easy, make it quick, open up without a kick."*

Jay ran at full speed and leaped to kick the door—just as it opened by itself. He landed on his butt inside the museum. Mal, Evie, and Carlos laughed and stepped over him.

"Coming?" Mal asked Jay, mocking him this time.

The gang passed the lobby and ran through the dark museum with Evie leading the way as she consulted her mirror. "Upstairs," she whispered to them.

They ran down a hall and up some stairs, then stopped short in a doorway to a room called the Gallery of Villains. On a pedestal, a wax figure of Evil Queen looked regal, sinister, and frightening— a powerful witch in her ultimate prime.

"Mommy?" said Evie, her mouth slack.

Jay looked up at a wax figure of Jafar, who wore full Arabian regalia, cobra staff raised above his head in a terrifying pose.

"Killer," said Jay, shaking his head.

Carlos gawked, terrified by the statue of Cruella with stone Dalmatians fleeing from her in terror. "I will never forget Mother's Day again," he said.

Mal stood in the shadow of what appeared to be a huge dragon. She looked up in awe at the most daunting and impressive display of all: Maleficent, calling upon the powers of hell. Mal remembered some of her mother's last words to her before she departed from the Isle of the Lost: *The future of the free world rests on your shoulders. Don't blow it.* Mal stared in shock and fear at her mom. Was this who she wanted to become?

"Well, the wand's not here," said Jay. "Let's bounce. Let's go!"

Evie and Carlos followed him back into the hall.

Mal lingered in the gallery. She couldn't take her eyes off her mother's statue. She took a few steps toward it. She imagined asking her mother what to do. In her mind, Maleficent sang to her about how they'd rule the world together, united in their evil ways. But Mal wasn't so sure that she wanted to rule the world anymore. . . .

"Hey!" said Evie with a smile.

Mal whipped around to face her.

"I found the wand!" said Evie. "Let's go!"

Mal took one more backward glance at Maleficent on the pedestal. She ran out after Evie and joined the gang. They looked down through an opening in the floor at the wand floating in a display. It was cream colored, long, and knobby.

"There it is!" said Evie.

The gang raced downstairs, past a room called the Hall of Castles, with Jay whooping and leading the way.

In the Wand Gallery, they approached its sole exhibit—Fairy Godmother's wand. It was lit from above and below with a soft blue light. Mal and her friends stopped at the threshold. Jay sized up the situation, making to pounce and grab it.

"Jay, don't!" said Mal, eying the blue light.

Again Jay moved to grab it.

"Wait, no! No! No! Don't!" said Mal.

Jay shot her a suave smile. He crawled into the exhibit, reached out, and . . .

Crack! Jay was blown back by a giant shock.

An alarm started to blare. Mal and her friends held their ears.

"A force field *and* a siren?" asked Carlos.

"That's just a little excessive," said Jay, regaining his stance.

Mal and her friends raced down the corridor. The alarm had woken the guard in the lobby, and he ran toward the noise. Little did Mal and her friends know he was just around the corner. Luckily, they ran in another direction. The group bolted for the exit, unseen, but Carlos stopped at the guard station. As his friends ran past Maleficent's spinning wheel and out the double doors, he assessed the equipment, looking for the alarm shutoff. The guard's phone rang.

Carlos answered it. "Hello? Uh, just give me one second, one second." He examined the guard's clipboard. "Uh, yeah, yeah. No, false alarm," he said.

"It was a malfunction in the LM 714 chip in the breadboard circuit. Yeah. Okay. Say hi to the missus." He hung up. The alarm stopped sounding. He looked up to see that the others had left without him. "You're welcome," he said to no one. He ran after his friends.

The four, empty-handed, sprinted through the night away from the museum.

"Way to go!" Mal said sarcastically. "Now we have to go to school tomorrow."

CHAPTER EIGHT

W E STILL DON'T HAVE THE WAND. GREAT. NOW WHAT?
GUESS WE'RE GOING TO HAVE TO SURVIVE SCHOOL
TILL WE FIGURE OUT A PLAN B. UGH!

The next morning, Fairy Godmother taught Mal and her friends about goodness.

She stood in front of a blackboard that had WEL-COME TO REMEDIAL GOODNESS! written on it, along with phrases like MOUTHS ARE FOR SMILING, NOT FOR BITING and SHARING IS CARING. Mal and her friends were the only kids enrolled in the class.

They were downright miserable.

"If someone hands you a crying baby," said Fairy Godmother, "do you: A. curse it, B. lock it in a tower, C. give it a bottle, or D. carve out its heart?"

Evie raised her hand enthusiastically.

"Evie!" said Fairy Godmother.

"What was the second one?" Evie asked.

"Oh, okay . . ." said Fairy Godmother. "Anyone else?"

Mal, who was sketching the wand, was called on. She looked up. "C. Give it a bottle," said Mal.

"Correct," said Fairy Godmother with a smile. "Again."

Jay sighed.

"You are on fire, girl!" said Carlos.

"Yeah!" said Evie.

"Just pick the one that doesn't sound like any fun," said Mal.

Her friends *ooh*ed.

"That makes so much sense," said Evie, starting to twirl her hair.

A girl in a pale blue dress with a big blue bow on her head entered the class. She cast a frightened look toward Mal and her friends and scurried toward Fairy Godmother at the blackboard. The girl held a clipboard in front of Fairy Godmother.

"Hello, dear one," said Fairy Godmother.

"Hi. You need to sign off on early dismissal for the coronation," the girl said.

Mal stopped sketching to study her.

"Everyone here remembers my daughter, Jane," said Fairy Godmother as she signed the form.

"Mom!" Jane whispered.

Jay and Carlos exchanged looks.

Fairy Godmother returned the clipboard to her daughter. "That's okay," she said, turning Jane to face Mal and her friends. "Jane, this is everyone."

Jane gave a feeble wave. "Hi. That's okay. Don't mind me. As you were," she said, bowing and rushing out of the room.

Mal smirked to herself.

"Forgive Jane," said Fairy Godmother. "I may have told her a few too many bedtime stories about your . . . parents." She cleared her throat. "Let's continue." She went back to the blackboard. "You find a vial of poison. Do you: A. put it in the king's wine, B. paint it on an apple, or C. turn it over to the proper authorities?"

Three hands shot up.

Carlos and Jay fought to be picked.

"Ooh! Ooh!" said Carlos.

"Jay," said Fairy Godmother.

"C. You turn it over to the proper authorities," said Jay coolly.

"I was gonna say that!" said Carlos.

Jay laughed mockingly. "But I said it first!" he said. He grabbed Carlos's head and put him in a headlock.

"Ow!" said Carlos.

"Who said it first?" said Jay. "Who said it first?"

He and Carlos started wrestling on top of their desk.

Evie put on lip gloss in her mirror. Mal sighed.

"Boys," said Fairy Godmother. Then she said it more loudly: "Boys!"

They froze.

"I am going to encourage you to use that energy on the tourney field," she said.

"Oh, no, that's okay. Whatever that is," said Carlos, "we'll pass."

But before he and Jay knew it, they were on the grassy green tourney field just outside the school. It resembled a lacrosse field but had two cannons at the fifty-yard line that shot a constant barrage of balls across the width of it. A big sign that read GO FIGHTING KNIGHTS! overlooked it. Jay and Carlos were barely recognizable in their tourney helmets and bucklers and multitude of pads.

The coach blew a whistle.

"Jay, Ben, offense," the referee instructed them. "Chad, you're defense!"

A handsome boy, Chad, strolled across the field.

"Hey! Hey! Put your helmet on! Get out of the kill zone!" the coach said to Carlos. "Pick it up! Put it on! Two hands!"

The coach blew the whistle again, and the play began. Jay was off like a shot. He ran right over Carlos, who thudded to the ground. Jay slammed his buckler into Chad, who had the ball. The ball flew free and Jay scooped it up. He charged down the field into the kill zone, roaring ferociously and dodging the flying balls expertly.

Carlos, meanwhile, was trying to crawl under the barrage of balls. Ben came to his rescue, batting the balls away as he pulled Carlos to his feet.

Jay slammed the ball right into the net. The cheerleaders whooped—all except for Audrey. Jay threw off his helmet and did a victory dance. Then he realized he was dancing alone. The field, he noticed, was littered with lots of penalty flags and battered, beaten, groaning players in both yellow and blue uniforms.

Coach blew his whistle. "You! Get over here!"

Jay trotted over to the coach, who stood among the downed players, Carlos included. Ben was hanging over his knees, panting.

"What do you call that?" yelled the coach.

Chad looked on smugly.

The coach's face broke into a smile. "I call that raw talent. Come find me later; I'll show you something you haven't seen before. It's called a rule book." He chuckled and patted Jay on the shoulder. "Welcome to the team, son!" He looked at Carlos and said, "You ever thought about band?"

Carlos tittered weakly and Jay laughed.

"I'll work with him, Coach," said Ben.

"All right," said the coach. "Let's run that again!" He blew his whistle, and the players moved to resume their positions on the field.

Jay grinned and spun around to find Chad glaring at him with his chin and nose stuck up in a rude, snobby way. Jay squinted at Chad and walked past him, bumping him hard. Once Jay had passed by, Chad rubbed his arm.

Mal and Evie parted ways at Mal's locker, which had EVIL LIVES spray-painted on it—a little something Mal did to make herself feel more at home.

Mal dug around in her locker. She heard loud, obnoxious laughter and looked up to see Audrey and Chad. Audrey wore pink sunglasses and a pale pink sweater. Chad wore his letter jacket. Ben appeared behind them in a smart-looking jacket.

"Those kids are trouble," Chad told Ben, pointing to Mal.

Audrey nodded, shooting Mal a particularly nasty look.

Mal turned away and tried to ignore them.

"Come on, Chad," said Ben. "Give them a chance."

Audrey took Ben's hands in hers. "Ugh! No offense, Bennybear—you're just too trusting," she said with a big smile. "Look, I know your mom fell in love with a big nasty beast who turned out to be a prince. But in *my* mom's story, the evil fairy was just the evil fairy." She nodded at Mal. "That girl's mother," she whispered.

"I think you're wrong about them," said Ben.

Audrey sighed, let him go, and walked off.

Ben approached Mal as she shut her locker. "Hey!" he said with a coy smile.

"Hey," she said, squinting at him.

"How's your first day?" he asked.

"Super," she said smugly.

"You should really think about taking this talent off the locker and into art class," Ben said. "I could sign you up. What do you think?" He gave her a long, intense look.

Mal spied Jane passing by them. "Way to take all the fun out of it," said Mal. She shot Ben a flirty smile, spun around with her spell book under her arm, and followed Jane into the bathroom, remembering the reason she was in Auradon in the first place: the wand. What better way to get close to it than through Jane?

Jane was alone at the bathroom mirror, looking at her short, straight brown bob. When she saw Mal enter, her eyes grew wide. She froze and then spun around.

"Hi!" said Mal brightly. "It's Jane, right? Always loved that name. Jane." She laughed.

"That's cool," said Jane, breaking her stare and making a beeline for the door.

Mal obstructed her way. "Don't go!"

Jane froze.

"I guess . . . I was just kind of hoping to make a friend," said Mal, putting on her most vulnerable voice. "You probably have all the friends you need, though, huh?"

"Hardly," said Jane.

Mal made herself sound surprised. "Really? I mean, with your mom being Fairy Godmother and headmistress. I mean, not to mention your own, um, I mean, your own"—she looked Jane up and down—"personality!" She giggled kindly.

"I'd rather be pretty," said Jane. "You've got great hair!"

Mal stroked her purple locks. "You know what? I have just the thing for that." She lifted her spell book and turned through the pages. "It's right . . . here!" She read from the page. *"Beware, forswear, replace the old with brand-new hair."*

With a few waves of Mal's finger, Jane suddenly had long, beautiful wavy brown locks. Jane gasped in delight as she studied her new do in the mirror.

"Wow! You almost don't notice your . . . other features anymore!" said Mal.

"Do my nose!" said Jane, turning to face her with a huge smile on her face.

"Oh, I can't. I wish I could," said Mal. "I've been practicing, but you know, I can't do really big magic. Not like your *mom*! With her *wand*! I mean, one *swoosh* from that thing and you could probably have whatever features you wanted."

Jane frowned. "She doesn't use the wand anymore. She believes the *real* magic is in books. And not the spell books. Regular books with history and stuff."

Mal laughed. "What a rip," she said. "You know, she used magic on Cinderella, who wasn't even her real daughter. Doesn't she love you?"

"Of course she does. It's just, you know, tough love," said Jane. "Work on the inside, not the outside. You know, that sort of thing . . ." She trailed off, looking sad.

"That's the face!" said Mal, pointing at Jane's sad expression. "Yeah! And then just look as if your heart is about to break." She pouted her lips and altered her voice to sound more like Jane. *"Oh, Mother, I just don't understand why you can't make me beautiful, too."* Her face broke into a grin.

"Think it would work?" asked Jane, blinking and smiling.

"Yeah! I mean, that's what old Cindy did. And your mother Bibbidi-Bobbidi-ed the living daylights out of *her*!" said Mal.

Jane laughed.

Mal's eyes flashed. "And, hey! If your mom does decide to break out the old wand . . . invite me! I just think it would be so . . . inspirational."

Jane smiled. "If I can convince Mom, you're so there!"

"Yay!" said Mal, clapping.

Jane took her purse and left the bathroom. "Bye," she said.

Mal smiled, pleased with herself. "Bye," she said.

CHAPTER NINE

JANE MAY BE MORE USEFUL TO US THAN I FIRST THOUGHT. HELLO, PLAN B!

ALSO, I LIKED HER SHORT HAIR BETTER. JUST SAYING.

In chemistry class, Evie sat next to Doug and stared longingly at Chad.

Across the lab bench, beyond the tubing, clamps, pipettes, and steaming beakers, Chad was bathed in his own golden light. Evie couldn't stop gazing at him. Chad tried to see what his lab partner was writing so he could copy the notes down.

The chemistry teacher, Mr. Delay, scribbled a formula on the chalkboard.

"Any chance he's in line for a throne?" Evie asked Doug. "*Anywhere* in line?"

"Chad. Prince Charming Jr., Cinderella's son," said Doug.

Evie turned and looked at Doug, then back at Chad.

"Chad inherited the charm, but not a lot of *there* there," said Doug. "Know what I mean?"

Evie rested her head on her hand. "Looks like there there to me," she said.

"Evie!" said Mr. Delay. "Perhaps this is just review for you. So tell me, what is the average atomic weight of silver?"

Evie stared at him blankly. "Atomic weight?" she said. "Uh . . . well . . . not very much. I mean, it's an atom, right?" She smiled and let out a laugh.

Chad laughed, too.

Mr. Delay beckoned her forth.

Evie pocketed her mirror and strolled confidently up to the chalkboard. "Let's see." She took the chalk from the teacher, stealthily removing her mirror and speaking down into it. "How do I find the average atomic weight of silver?" She glanced at her mirror, hidden at her side, and it revealed the whole long calculation of the answer, which she copied onto the chalkboard. "That would be 106.905 times .5200 plus 108.905 times .4800, which, Mr. Delay, would give us 107.9 amu." She smiled.

Chad, impressed, copied her calculation into his lab notebook.

Doug looked at Evie curiously. *"Amu?"* he mouthed to himself.

"It was a mistake to underestimate—" said Mr. Delay.

Evie spun around in a circle, whipping the teacher with her long blue-black locks. "A villain?" she said, smiling. "Don't make it again." She threw him the chalk and flounced back toward her seat. As she passed Chad, he slipped her a note and ogled her. When Evie sat down, she opened the note. It read MEET ME UNDER THE BLEACHERS AT 3. She looked up at Chad and nodded at him. He rested his head on his hand, and Evie did the same. They locked eyes and shared a dreamy, longing look.

Doug rested his head on his hand, too, and frowned.

~~~

On the grassy tourney field, Ben stood with a stop-watch, facing Carlos.

"Okay, Carlos," said Ben. "We're gonna do some sprints. Ready?"

Carlos, who was kneeling a good distance away, nodded at him.

A little dog came out of nowhere, barking, and began to chase Carlos, who took off. Carlos sped toward Ben, then past him, screaming in terror. *"Ahhh!"*

Ben clicked his watch. "Sweet!" Then he realized Carlos was being chased.

Carlos kept running. He ran into the woods, the dog hot on his heels. He hopped partway up a tree, and the dog stood at its base, watching him. "No! Stop!" he shouted, terrified.

The scruffy rust-colored dog looked up at him with wide imploring eyes.

"Carlos!" Ben called.

"Ben! Ben? Ben, help me!" Carlos shouted as Ben appeared. "This thing is a killer! He's gonna chase me down and rip out my throat! This is a vicious rabid pack animal!"

"Hey, who told you that?" asked Ben, lifting the little dog.

"My mother," said Carlos.

"Cruella?" asked Ben.

"She's a dog expert. A 'dog yellerer,' " said Carlos.

Ben's face broke into a smile.

"Why are you holding him? He's gonna attack you!" said Carlos.

"Carlos, you've never actually met a dog, have you?" said Ben.

"Of course not," said Carlos.

"Dude, meet Carlos. Carlos, this is Dude. He's the campus mutt," said Ben.

"He doesn't look like a rabid pack animal," said Carlos, stepping down from the tree. "Geez, it's kind of like looking into a mirror." Carlos spoke to Dude. "I bet you're used to being kicked around, right?" Carlos scratched Dude's head and smiled.

Ben smiled, too, and passed Dude over to Carlos.

"You're a good boy," said Carlos, laughing and rubbing Dude's belly.

Ben's smile faded. "I guess you guys have it pretty rough on the island," he said.

"Yeah," said Carlos. "Let's just say we don't get a lot of belly rubs."

Ben unconsciously patted Carlos on the shoulder. "Good boy," he said. He caught himself. "I mean, you're a good runner. You're fast."

Carlos smiled. "Thank you."

"Yeah," said Ben. "Listen, I'm gonna give you guys some space. You guys get to know each other and just come find me when you're done, okay?" Ben started to walk away, back toward the tourney field.

"Okay," said Carlos.

"See you later," said Ben.

"See you out there," said Carlos.

Once Ben had disappeared down the trail, Carlos sat down on a log with Dude on his lap. He scratched the dog's side. Dude licked him playfully on the nose.

"Oh!" said Carlos, glad he'd made a new friend. "Thank you!"

Chad led Evie under the bleachers and they stood facing each other.

"Is everybody at home as pretty as you?" Chad asked her, shouldering a huge tan backpack.

Evie looked down at her shoes and blushed. "I like to think I'm the fairest of them all." She batted her eyelashes and laughed. "How many rooms in your castle?"

Chad smiled. "Too many to count."

Evie leaned in to kiss Chad. He leaned in, too, but he stopped abruptly.

Evie smooched air.

"You *really* nailed that chemistry problem today!" he said. "You're going to have all the nerds in love with you." He laughed.

"I'm not that smart!" said Evie.

"Oh, come on," said Chad.

"No, really! I'm not. But I'm really good at sewing and cooking and cleaning. You know, like your mother, Cinderella. Without the ratty dress," she said. She took the mirror out of her purse. "See this? If I ask it where something is, it tells me."

"Are you kidding me?" asked Chad, snatching it from her hand. He spoke into the mirror with a hardened, demanding voice. "Where's my cell phone?" he barked.

"It won't work for you, silly." Evie laughed.

"No biggie," said Chad, handing it back to her and resuming his charming act. "My dad will just get me a new one."

"Prince Charming," said Evie dreamily.

"Yeah," said Chad, smiling.

"And Cinderella," said Evie.

"Yeah," said Chad.

"Fairy Godmother." She took Chad's hands in hers. "Hey, I heard her wand is in some boring museum. Do they always leave it there?" She looked deeply into his eyes and leaned forward as if she were about to kiss him.

He started to lean in again but stopped once more. "I'd really like to talk, but"—he turned away dramatically—"I'm just swamped!" he said. "Unless . . ." He turned back to face her.

"Unless?" asked Evie with a smile.

"If you could knock all my homework out along with yours, then maybe we could get together sometime and . . . hang." His eyebrows jumped. He took off his backpack and handed it to her.

"Okay," she said breathily, taking it.

"Thanks, babe," he said, winking at her. He walked off.

"Bye," said Evie dreamily, waving.

Suddenly, Doug's face appeared between the seats of the bleachers.

"I couldn't help but overhear—"

"Are you *stalking me*?" Evie said.

"Technically . . . yes," said Doug. "I, too, have a fascination with Fairy Godmother's wand." He climbed down from the bleachers and stood in front of Evie. "Which is another reason I look forward to the coronation. Perhaps we could sit next to each other and discuss its attributes." His voice cracked.

"Are you saying they use it in the coronation?" asked Evie, resting a finger on Doug's chest right below his green bow tie.

"Yes," said Doug. Then he added, "And asking you out."

Evie laughed in his face flirtatiously and walked away, ignoring his request for a date.

Doug, enchanted, watched as Evie strutted back to the dorms.

CHAPTER TEN

I T'S TIME TO GIVE THIS PLAID PREPPY SCHOOL A SERIOUS
BAD-GIRL MAKEOVER.

In Mal and Evie's dorm room, Jane and Mal spoke as Evie sewed on her machine.

The sun shone into the room and fell across Mal's sketchbook. She was lying on her bed, shading in a drawing of Beast as Jane stood clutching the bedpost.

"Mom said, '*If a boy can't see the beauty within, then he's not worth it,*'" Jane mimicked in a singsong voice. "Can you believe it? What world does she live in?" She stomped angrily across the room.

Mal snickered. "Auradon?" she muttered.

Evie held up the dress she'd been sewing. "Mal? Do you like?"

Mal looked up. "Yeah. It's cute. It brings out your eyes," she said.

"I know," said Evie, smiling. She started to sew again.

"I'll never get a boyfriend," Jane said. She flopped down on Evie's bed.

"*Boyfriends* are overrated," Mal said.

"And how would you know, Mal?" said Evie. "You've never had one."

"It's 'cause I don't need one, *E*," said Mal. "They're a waste of time."

Evie gasped. "I forgot to do Chad's homework!" she said. She stood up. "Oh, no. Oh, no, no, no, no!" She grabbed Chad's backpack and sat again at her sewing desk.

Mal said, "And that is *exactly* what I mean."

There was a knock on the door and a girl stepped into the room. She wore a pink floral shirt with a pink sash and a short teal skirt. She sported a short bob hairstyle with bangs. "Hey, guys! I'm Lonnie!"

the girl said brightly. She eyed Mal and Evie. "My mom's Mulan . . . ?"

They gave her blank stares. Evie took a binder out of Chad's backpack.

"No? Anyways!" said Lonnie. "I *love* what you've done with Jane's hair. And I know you hate us. And, well, you're evil. . . . But do you think you could do mine?" She touched her bob.

Mal scoffed. "Why would I do that for you?" she asked.

"I'll pay you fifty dollars," said Lonnie, holding out a silk bag of money.

"Good answer," said Evie, taking the bag and standing. "I need to buy more material." She squinted at Lonnie. "Let's see. I'm thinking we lose the bangs . . . maybe some layers . . . and some highlights!"

"Um . . . no, no. I want it cool," said Lonnie. "Like Mal's!"

Mal looked at Lonnie with her jaw dropped.

Evie laughed. "Really?" she said. "The split ends, too?"

Mal rolled her eyes and let out an exasperated breath. She put down her pencil, got up, and opened her spell book. "Okay . . ." she said, flipping through it. She smiled at Lonnie. *"Beware, forswear, replace the old with cool hair,"* she said. With a few swipes of Mal's finger, Lonnie's bob transformed into long, soft brown locks.

Lonnie checked herself out in the mirror and frowned.

"I know, I know," said Evie, going over to her. "It looks like a mop on your head. Let's cut it off, layer it—"

"No, no, no, no, no!" said Lonnie. "I love it." She smiled.

"You do," said Evie.

"It's just . . ." She ripped her skirt up the side. "Now I'm cool," she said.

"Like ice," said Mal, flashing her a smile.

And with that, a little friendship was born.

Jane looked between the two and ripped her skirt up the side, too. She instantly gasped. "What did I just do?" Jane said. "Mom's gonna kill me!"

~~~

Jay and Coach Jenkins were seated on the bleachers, looking at the rule book.

"I could really use a tough guy like you," said Coach Jenkins. He looked very official in a yellow tourney hat, a blue vest, and a pale yellow T-shirt. There was a jersey slung over his shoulder. "The team's a bunch of princes, if you know what I mean," he added.

"You're telling me," said Jay, closing the rule book. "It's all *After you, old chum. Oh, pardon me, did I bump you?'*"

Coach chuckled.

"Where I come from, it's *'Prepare to die, sucker!'*" Jay threw down the rule book and stood up. "As my father says, the only way to win is to make sure everyone else loses! You rip—"

"Jay," Coach said. He stood up. "Jay! Jay, Jay, Jay. Let me explain a 'team.'" He guided Jay to sit back down on the bleachers with him. "It's like a family," Coach said.

"You do *not* want to be at my house at dinner-time," said Jay.

Coach nodded. "Okay, okay," he said. "You

know how a body has a lot of different parts? Legs, elbows, ears. But they all need each other. Well, that's what a team is—different players who work *together* to win. Make any sense?"

Jay looked thoughtful. "Can I be the fist?" He made a fist.

Coach laughed. He took the jersey off his shoulder and held it out to Jay.

It was blue and had Jay's name and the number eight on it in gold.

With a smile, Jay took it and put it on over his leather vest. He thanked Coach Jenkins and took off down the field and back to the dorms. He threw open the door to Mal and Evie's room, whooping and showing off his jersey. Carlos whistled from where he sat with Dude on the floor, looking at something on his laptop. Evie was bending over a mountain of homework and copying two sets of answers from her magic mirror. Mal leafed through the spell book on her bed, searching for answers.

"Did your plan work with Jane?" Jay asked Mal. "Are you going over to see the wand?"

"Do you think that I would be going through

every single spell in this book if I hadn't completely struck out?" said Mal.

Her friends exchanged looks.

"Someone is in a bad mood," said Carlos.

"My mom's counting on me," said Mal, flicking Carlos's head. "I can't let her down!"

"We can do this!" said Jay.

His three friends stared at him.

"If we stick together," said Jay.

"And we won't go back until we do," said Mal. "'Cause we're rotten . . ."

"To the core," they all said in unison.

"Oh, yeah," said Evie nonchalantly. "I found out that Fairy Godmother blesses Ben with the wand at coronation and we all get to go."

Mal's eyes widened.

"I have nothing to wear, of course," said Evie.

Mal looked at her incredulously.

There was a knock at the door.

"What?" asked Evie.

"Hold that thought," Mal told Evie. She got up and opened the door.

Ben stood in the hall, smiling. "Hey, Mal!" he

said. "I didn't see you guys today. I was just wondering if you had any questions or anything . . . that you needed?"

"Not that I can think of. . . ." Mal looked at her friends, then back at Ben.

"Okay! All right! Well, if you need anything . . ." he said, starting off down the hall.

"Oh! Wait!" said Mal.

Ben paused.

"Um, is it true that we all get to go to your coronation?" asked Mal.

Ben smiled. "Yeah, the whole school goes."

"Wow. That is beyond exciting," said Mal. "Do you think it is at all a possibility that the four of us could stand in the front row next to the Fairy Godmother just so we could . . . soak up all that goodness?"

Ben looked like he was about to say yes, but his face fell. "I wish you could. Up in front it's just me, my folks, and my girlfriend."

"And your girlfriend," said Mal, nodding slowly.

"Yeah," said Ben. "I'm sorry."

"Okay, thanks, bye," said Mal, shutting the door in his face. She turned to her friends and smiled mischievously. "I think it's time that Bennyboo got himself a new girlfriend. And I need a love spell." She clapped and Carlos tossed her the spell book.

CHAPTER ELEVEN

INITIATE PLAN C: THE LOVE SPELL.
WHAT COULD POSSIBLY GO WRONG?

Mal whisked together the ingredients for the love spell in the kitchen of the school.

Her three friends hung out around her.

"You want a treat, Dude?" Carlos said. He pulled a snack out of the fridge and walked it over to the rust-colored pooch, who sat in a bowl on the stove top.

"Okay," Mal said to herself as she referenced the spell book.

Evie scampered over, carrying a bowl of walnuts.

Mal incanted, stirring the contents of the large metal bowl. *"Crush his heart with an iron glove by making him a slave to love,"* she said. Then she turned to Evie. "Um, all right. It says that we still need one tear." Mal pouted and said, "I never cry."

"Let's just chop up some onions," said Carlos, holding up an onion.

"No!" said Mal. "It says that we need one tear of human sadness. This love potion gets the best reviews, so we have to follow it exactly."

"A tear's a tear," said Jay.

"That's not true, Jay," said Evie. "They both have antibodies and enzymes, but an emotional tear has more protein-based hormones than a reflex tear."

Mal grinned. "Listen to you," she said.

Evie beamed.

"Yeah, I knew that," said Jay.

"Did not," said Carlos, tapping his arm.

"Yeah, I did," said Jay.

The kitchen door opened. Lonnie appeared in bright pink floral pajamas.

"There you are, Mal!" said Lonnie, walking toward her.

Mal hid the spell book under a kitchen towel.

"I was looking for you! You know, all the girls want you to do their hair!" She looked from Mal to

MAL SHOWED OFF HER ART SKILLS BY SPRAY-PAINTING A WALL.

Evie, Jay, Mal, and Carlos roamed the streets of the Isle of the Lost, trying to think of new ways to be bad.

When Maleficent described her plans for world domination, Mal felt a mix of fear and admiration for her mother.

Audrey held Ben's arm possessively. She wanted everyone to know he was her "Bennyboo."

Carlos and Jay had a lot to learn in Remedial Goodness class.

When Jay tried playing tourney, he found out he was a natural.

After Mal recited, "Beware, forswear, replace the old with brand-new hair," Jane had long wavy locks!

EVIE GAZED LONGINGLY AT CHAD. "ANY CHANCE HE'S IN LINE FOR A THRONE?" SHE ASKED DOUG.

WHEN CHAD ASKED EVIE TO MEET HIM UNDER THE BLEACHERS, SHE THOUGHT SHE HAD SCORED HER PRINCE. UNFORTUNATELY, HE HAD OTHER PLANS.

Lonnie couldn't believe Mal's and her friends' parents had never made chocolate chip cookies for them.

Dude the dog sat in a bowl and watched the kids prepare the magic cookies that would make Ben fall in love with Mal.

Mal tried to save Ben from drowning even though she didn't know how to swim.

The highlight of Family Day for Carlos and Jay? The chocolate fountain.

"Evie, you will use this to take the driver out," said Mal.

Ben munched the cupcake. "Mmm, this is really good."

Evie to Carlos and Jay. Then she looked at the bowl in front of Mal. "Midnight snack, huh? Whatcha guys making?"

"Nothing special," said Mal. "Just cookies."

Lonnie swiped a taste of dough from the bowl.

"No! Wait!" Mal and her friends shouted in unison.

Lonnie licked her finger with gusto.

Everyone stared at her.

Lonnie looked from person to person. "What? I'm not going to double dip."

"Feel anything?" asked Evie.

"Yeah, like it's missing something?" said Mal, studying her.

Jay tossed his hair and gave Lonnie his most dashing smile, planting himself in front of her. "Hey, there."

Lonnie gave him a blank stare. "Could use some chips," she said, heading over to the refrigerator and opening the door.

Jay looked stung.

"And those are . . . ?" asked Mal.

"Chocolate chips. Just *the* most important food

group." Lonnie set a bowl of chocolate chips down on the table. She noticed their blank stares and said, "Wait. Didn't your moms ever make you guys chocolate chip cookies? Like when you're feeling sad, and they're fresh from the oven with a big old glass of milk and she makes you laugh and puts everything into perspective and . . ." Her voice trailed off.

Mal and her friends stared at Lonnie as if she were speaking another language.

"Why are you all looking at me like that?" Lonnie asked them.

"It's just different where we're from," said Mal.

"Yeah, I know," said Lonnie. "I just, I thought . . . even villains love their kids."

Mal and her friends did not look at one another.

They were all lost in a real glimpse of what they'd been missing.

"How awful," said Lonnie. Tears welled in her eyes at the thought. She touched Mal's hand in a comforting way. Mal watched as a fat tear rolled down Lonnie's cheek. Mal quickly wiped it away, surreptitiously flicking it into the dough.

"Yeah, well, big bummer, but we have to get these into the oven, so thank you so much for coming by. Really, really, have a good night," said Mal, guiding Lonnie toward the door.

Evie mixed the dough furiously.

"See you tomorrow. Evil dreams," Mal said, waving.

"Good night!" said Lonnie, ducking out of the kitchen.

Mal turned toward her friends. "Okay!" She clapped. "Boys. Cookie sheets!"

They loaded the dough onto the sheets and waited till the cookies were done and cooled before transferring them to a baggie and heading to their dorms to sleep.

The next morning, Mal and Jay walked through the school and outside by the lockers, following Ben and Audrey at a careful distance. A group of girls with fun, edgy hairdos were hanging out at a picnic table nearby. When they saw Mal, they waved and pointed to their new looks. Mal waved back at them and opened her locker. Jay noticed Mal pulling out her baggie with a special love-spell cookie inside.

"Are you feeling kind of weird about this?" he asked her. "I mean, it's not so bad here." He laughed.

Mal faced him. "Are you insane? Long live evil!" She shook her fist. "You're mean! You're awful!" She pointed a finger. "You're *bad news*! Snap out of it!" She snapped twice.

Jay said, "Thanks, Mal. I needed that." He laughed and walked toward the picnic table of girls, who ran over to him. "Hello," he said to them. "The name's Jay. Y'all going to the tourney game tonight?" The girls giggled flirtatiously.

"Do you think they actually paid for those?" Mal heard Audrey ask Ben, pointing to the girls' new hairstyles. Audrey turned petulantly to Ben. "She did it to Jane's hair, too, and Fairy Godmother's not happy about it. Isn't that breaking rules? I mean really, Ben, what did you expect?"

"What's the harm?" asked Ben, shrugging.

"It's gateway magic!" said Audrey. "Sure, it starts with the hair. Next thing you know, it's the lips and the legs and the clothes, and then everybody looks good, and then where will *I* be?" She pointed to herself.

"Listen, Audrey—" Ben started.

She composed herself. "I will see you at the game after my dress fitting for the coronation, okay? Bye, Bennyboo." She air-kissed his cheek and flounced off.

Mal slammed the door of her locker. "Hey, Bennyboo!"

"Hey!" He smiled and walked over to her.

"I just made a batch of cookies." Mal held up the baggie to him with an innocent look on her face. "Double chocolate chip. Do you want one?"

"I've got a big game. I don't eat before a big game," said Ben. "But thank you so, so much. Thank you. Next time, next time." He started to walk away.

Mal smiled and nodded. "No, yeah, I completely understand," she said. "Be careful of treats offered by kids of villains. I'm sure every kid in Auradon knows that."

"That's not it," said Ben. "No, no, no."

"No, I get it. You're cautious. That's smart. Oh,

well. More for me, I guess," said Mal. She took the cookie from the baggie and acted like she was about to take a bite.

Ben grabbed it and scarfed it down. "See that? Totally trust you," he said. "Totally."

Mal glanced over her shoulder at her friends, then back at Ben. "How was it?" she asked.

"Good. Great. Amazing! I mean, it's chewy. Mmm . . . Is that walnuts?"

Mal nodded.

"I love walnuts," he said. "I mean, the chocolate . . ." He cleared his throat and his eyes focused completely on Mal. "The chocolate chips. I'm sorry. They're warm . . . soft. . . . They're sweet." He looked deeper into Mal's eyes. "Mal, have you always had those little golden flecks in your eyes?"

Jay, Carlos, and Evie crept close to Mal and Ben.

Jay clapped his hand on Ben's shoulder. "How you feeling, bro?" he asked.

Mal looked at Ben, pleased that the spell seemed to be working.

"I feel like singing your name!" Ben told her. "*Mal!*"

Mal looked horrified and clamped a hand over his mouth.

"Let's get you to the game," said Jay, steering Ben away.

Evie and Carlos shot Mal a look. Mal gulped and smiled.

CHAPTER TWELVE

TOURNEY IS A FUN GAME.
  SO IS RUINING LIVES.

On the tourney field, the Fighting Knights and the Sherwood Falcons were tied.

The scoreboard read 2:2 with forty-seven seconds left on the clock. Cheerleaders, including Audrey, clapped, chanted, and danced. Jane, the mascot, in a knight's suit of armor, jumped up and down with them. An announcer stood on the field with a golden microphone, as the teams got into their huddles and took up positions along the kill zones. Mal and Evie stood in the bleachers, watching Jay and Carlos down on the bench.

Coach looked at Jay. "You're up!" he said.

Jay grabbed Carlos. "Coach!" he said. "How about my buddy here?"

"Hmmm, not so sure about that," said Carlos.

"Coach, he's been practicing," said Jay. "And you said yourself a team was made up of a bunch of parts."

"Jay, I'm not that good," said Carlos.

"Well, he's kind of like my brain," said Jay.

Coach called Amir, another player, off the field. Then he turned to Carlos and tossed him his playing stick. "You heard him!" he barked at Carlos. "Get out there!"

"Don't worry, bro. I got your back," said Jay.

Carlos gulped. "How about my front?"

Jay laughed and gave him a friendly noogie.

Jay and Carlos trotted out onto the field and took their positions.

The announcer said, "He's bringing Jay in from the Isle of the Lost and that little guy Carlos who can barely hold his shield! And the tip-off is ready. Here we go."

The girls in the stands and the cheerleaders squealed in glee at the sight of Jay suited up. The teams broke from their huddles. The long pass went to Jay. Jay dished it off to Ben. Carlos blocked a player and did a little jig in his opponent's face. Jay, who was in possession of the ball again, did a hurdling maneuver midfield. He made a nice pass to Ben, who was in the kill zone. Chad did a big block, then passed the ball to Jay. Now Jay was in the clear. He shot the ball, but it was saved by the Falcons' goalkeeper.

"Come on, guys!" shouted Coach Jenkins from the sidelines.

"Twenty-three seconds left," boomed the announcer. "You could cut the tension with a sword!"

The next play began. The long ball was passed to Jay, who leaped and ran with it down the field. There was a big block from Chad. Jay dished the ball off to Ben. Carlos, with a big block, went down. Jay ran through the kill zone and picked up Carlos. They were hammered by dragon fire. Jay did another hurdling maneuver midfield and ran until he was in the clear and could get the ball again.

"Jay!" called Carlos, who stood in front of the goal.

"Carlos!" said Jay, whipping the ball his way. The ball bounced off Carlos and flew back to Jay, who passed it to Ben. Ben shot and scored. The Knights had won.

In the stands, the crowd roared and went wild. Mal held her ears.

"What a team!" said the announcer. "Incredible! And it's the new guys, Jay and Carlos, who set up the prince for the win. What a victory! An absolutely wonderful end to one of the best games ever! Here they come, folks, the winners—"

Ben grabbed the microphone out of the announcer's hands and said, "Excuse me! Excuse me! Can I have your attention, please?"

The crowd went silent.

He stood on the dragon cannon. "There's something I'd like to say!"

Mal watched him from the bleachers with wide eyes.

Ben surveyed his captive audience. "Gimme an *M*!" he shouted, making his arms form the letter *M*.

There was an echo from the crowd after the letter. They all copied his moves.

"Gimme an *A*!" said Ben, arms at his sides.

"A!" roared the crowd.

"Gimme an *L*!" said Ben, throwing his arms up.

"L!" boomed the crowd.

"What does that spell?" asked Ben.

"Mal!" said the audience.

Mal crossed her arms and looked mortified.

"Come on, I can't hear you!" said Ben.

"Mal!" the crowd roared.

"I love you, Mal," Ben said. "Did I mention that?"

Mal pursed her lips and grinned.

Audrey, looking heartbroken, ran off the field.

The crowd *ooohe*d.

Ben turned to the band. "Gimme a beat!" he said.

The band churned out a funky rhythm. The whole crowd, with the exception of Mal, joined in as Ben led an R & B stomp out on the field. Mal smiled and blushed. With Carlos, Jay, and Chad as his backup, Ben began to sing a song to Mal. He danced and sang about how his love for her was ridiculous. Mal put her hands over her mouth.

She couldn't help smiling as Ben shook and rolled in the grass and knocked his knees together. He took off his sweaty jersey, balled it up, and tossed it to swooning girls in the bleachers. Mal surprised herself and leaped to catch it. Ben crowd-surfed up into the bleachers so that he stood right in front of Mal, who clutched his jersey like it was made of gold.

The band stopped playing and everyone clapped.

Ben moved in to kiss Mal, but she blocked his attempt with a squeal.

"I love you, Mal. Did I mention that?" Ben asked, pulling Mal into a side hug.

Audrey and Chad climbed the bleachers and leaped up beside them.

Audrey snatched the microphone out of Ben's hands. "Chad's my boyfriend now!" she said, draping her arm around Chad. "And I'm going to the coronation with him. So I don't need your pity date." She smiled and kissed Chad firmly on the lips.

Evie put her hands on her hips and looked away.

Ben grabbed the microphone back. "Mal!" he

said. "Will you go to the coronation with me?"

"Yes!" Mal said into the microphone with a huge smile.

"She said yes!" Ben announced.

People in the stands cheered.

Audrey huffed, and she and Chad stormed off.

Jay appeared beside Ben. "Come on, man. Whole team's waiting for you!"

"Bye," said Mal.

Ben and Jay ran down to the field.

Mal squealed to herself and checked out Ben's jersey in her hands. She bit her lips and shrugged. She looked at Evie and saw that her best friend looked awfully upset.

"I feel *really* sorry for Audrey," said Mal.

Evie looked surprised. "You do?"

"Yeah. I feel like if she were talented like you, and she knew how to sew and do triple flips, then she wouldn't need a prince to make her feel better about herself."

Evie chuckled softly and smiled. "I guess I am kind of gifted," she said.

"Kind of," said Mal, smiling.

Evie laughed and beamed at Mal. "Thanks, M," she said.

Below, the players on the field whooped. Mal and Evie waved at them as Jay held the trophy over his head and his teammates lifted him up on their shoulders.

CHAPTER THIRTEEN

MAYBE THE WHOLE LOVE SPELL THING WASN'T SUCH A BAD IDEA AFTER ALL. . . .

In chemistry, Evie and her classmates were taking a tough multipage test.

Chad tried to cheat off another student, who blocked his view. Evie frowned at a hard problem. She gave up and reached for the mirror in her purse.

But it wasn't there.

"Looking for something?" asked Mr. Delay, holding up her mirror.

Evie gasped, speechless.

"Thank you, Chad," said Mr. Delay, resting a hand on his shoulder. "It's gratifying to see someone still respects the honor code."

Chad looked at her smugly.

Evie glared at him.

Mr. Delay rounded on Evie. "It will be my recommendation that you are expelled," he said.

Doug stood beside her in protest. "That isn't fair!" he said. "Obviously she wasn't cheating, since she didn't have that . . . whatever it is."

"It's called a magic mirror—" said Evie.

"Not helping," Doug whispered to her.

"Okay, sorry," said Evie, bowing her head.

"Maybe she needed another pencil," he told the teacher.

"Actually, I was—" Evie started.

"Really," Doug told Evie. "Don't help." He turned to the teacher. "Please."

"Please," said Evie, looking up at Mr. Delay.

"Well, if you can pass this test, I'll return your property and let the matter drop," said Mr. Delay.

Evie smiled and Doug sighed.

Chad smiled meanly at her.

She smiled right back at him.

A little while later, Evie ran up to Doug, who was at a picnic table outside doing his homework and eating lunch. She placed her blue Auradon Prep examination booklet in front of him. There was a red "B+" at the top of the booklet.

"For the first time, it's like I'm more than just a pretty face," Evie said.

Doug laughed. "Shocker, huh?" he said with a warm smile.

Evie took a seat beside him. "You were pretty great in there," she said.

Doug grinned dopily. "So were you."

Evie beamed. "I bet I can get an A on the next test without the mirror," she said.

"Maybe we can get together and hang out," said Doug.

"Yeah," said Evie, blushing. "Let's get together!"

Mal appeared beside them. "There you are!" she said. "I have been looking for you literally everywhere." She slammed her hands down on the picnic table.

"What's wrong?" asked Evie.

"Ben just asked me out on"—Mal huffed—"a *date*!"

Evie and Doug chuckled.

"We can handle this," Evie told her with a devious smile. She looked at Doug. "Bye!" she told him. She stood up and turned to Mal. "You're looking a little pale, but I can fix that with a lip gloss and some blush—"

"No, no, no . . ." said Mal as the girls headed back to their dorm.

Before Mal knew it, she was seated on her bed in the dorm room as Evie applied blush to her cheeks, making them rosy. She was dressed for her date in a terrific mix of punk and princess, with a scarf, dress, and leather jacket.

"Okay! Easy on the blush!" said Mal. "I don't want to scare him away." She looked thoughtful and smiled. "Not that I could," she added.

"Please," said Evie. "Mom taught me how to apply blush before I could talk." She carefully finished applying the color. "Always use upward strokes."

"My mom was never really big on makeup tips," said Mal. "I never had a sister."

"Well, now you do," said Evie, dabbing red lipstick on Mal's lips. "We're gonna need all the family we can get if we don't pull this off. My mother's not a barrel of laughs when she doesn't get her way." Evie rolled her eyes. "Just ask Snow White."

"Are you afraid of her?" asked Mal.

"Sometimes," said Evie. "Are you afraid of your mom?"

"I just really want her to be proud of me," said Mal. "She gets so angry with me when I disappoint her. And, yeah, she's my mom, so I know she loves me . . . in her own way."

Evie took her hand and smiled. "Moving on," she said. "Come see."

"Are we done?" asked Mal.

"Yeah," said Evie as she led Mal to the mirror.

Mal looked at herself and laughed.

Evie hugged her. "I know," said Evie.

"I look . . ." said Mal.

"Say it," said Evie.

"Not hideous," said Mal.

"Not even close," said Evie, shaking her head and beaming.

Mal giggled and broke into a radiant smile.

Just then, there was a knock at the door.

CHAPTER FOURTEEN

My date with Ben is about to begin.
    Is it weird that I'm kind of extremely looking forward to it? Shhh!

When Mal opened the door, she looked into the face of Ben.

He wore his letter jacket and carried two helmets. "For the first time, I understand the difference between pretty and beautiful," he said.

Mal's face broke into a smile.

"I hope you like bikes," he said to Mal, offering her a helmet. Mal took the helmet and shot Evie a look as she stepped out.

Evie grinned and closed the door.

Mal walked with Ben down the hall and outside

the school, where Ben's Vespa was waiting for them. She and Ben hopped onto it and sped off, cruising down a paved road. Mal, grinning ear to ear, held on to Ben's chest as they rode through the beautiful countryside. Sunlight dappled ferns and trees, and birds chirped.

Before Mal knew it, they were slowing through a grove of tall trees. Ben parked the Vespa and kicked the stand down. He helped Mal off it and began leading her through the forest and onto a suspension bridge high above a rushing stream.

"Tell me something about yourself that you've never told anyone," Ben said.

"Um . . . my middle name is . . . Bertha," said Mal.

"Bertha?" Ben asked.

"Yeah," said Mal.

"Bertha," said Ben.

"Just my mom doing what she does best," said Mal. "Being really, *really* evil."

Ben laughed.

"Mal Bertha," said Mal.

"Mine's Florian," said Ben.

"Florian? How princely," said Mal. "Oh, that's almost worse." She laughed.

"I mean, you know, it's better than Bertha, but it's still not good," said Ben.

They finished crossing the bridge.

Ben grinned at her. "Close your eyes," he said.

Mal closed her eyes and allowed Ben to guide her down a forest path. He took her hands and pulled her gently this way and that, over logs and across puddles.

Finally, he stopped. "You ready?" he asked her.

Mal nodded.

"Open," he said.

Mal opened her eyes.

Ben had brought her to the Enchanted Lake. It was all that and more: Mal looked upon a magical lake that was the color of jade. Into the lake jutted a stone platform with a few ancient pillars wrapped in ivy with purple flowers. Mal gasped at the beauty of it. Ben smiled at her, and she smiled back.

They walked onto the platform, where a blue

picnic blanket and a lavish array of food had been laid out for them, and they sat down.

Mal took a jelly doughnut and scarfed it down. She got powdered sugar on her face as she finished it.

"Is this your first time?" asked Ben.

"Mmm . . . We don't really . . . date much on the island. It's more like . . . gang activity," said Mal. She licked the sugar off her fingers.

Ben laughed. "I meant is this your first time eating a jelly doughnut," said Ben with a smile.

"Is it bad?" she asked.

"You've got a . . ." He leaned forward to brush the sugar from her lips.

"Gone?" Mal licked her lips. "Can't take me anywhere, I guess," she said.

Ben chuckled. "You know, I've done all the talking," he said. "Your turn. I really don't know that much about you." He leaned close to her. "Tell me something."

"Well . . ." Mal let out a sigh. "I'm sixteen. I'm an only child. And I've only ever lived in one place."

"Me too! We have so much in common already!" Ben said.

"No," said Mal. She laughed. "Trust me. We do not." Her smile faded. "And now you're going to be king."

Ben looked down.

"What?" asked Mal.

"A crown doesn't make you a king," said Ben.

Mal squinted. "Well, it kind of does." She laughed.

Ben smiled. "Your mother is Mistress of Evil. I've got the poster parents for goodness," said Ben. "But we're not automatically like them. We get to choose who we're going to be. And right now, I can look into your eyes and I can tell you're not evil. I can see." He stared intently into Mal's eyes. His gaze seemed to bore into her soul.

Mal was afraid of what he might see in her eyes.

Ben looked at the lake. "Let's go for a swim!" he said.

"What? Right now?" asked Mal.

Ben stood and held out his hand. "Come on. Yeah, right now."

Mal glanced at the water. "I think I'm just gonna stay here," she said.

"No, no, no, no. Come on," said Ben. His hand reached for Mal.

"I think I'm gonna stay behind and try a strawberry." Mal grabbed one from a bowl. "I've literally never tried a strawberry before." She took a big bite. "Mmmmm."

Ben chuckled. "Don't eat all of them," he said.

"Okay," said Mal, grabbing two more.

Ben walked away. Mal continued to chow down.

When Mal looked over her shoulder, she saw he'd climbed one of the large rocks surrounding the lake and perched near its top. He looked cute, even though his swim trunks had crowns on them.

He waved at her.

Mal stood. "Are those little crowns on your shorts?" she called.

He looked down at his swim trunks. "Maybe," he said, smiling. Then, with a beastly roar, Ben cannonballed off the rock and made a gigantic splash in the lake.

Mal's face glowed. She had a million thoughts in her head; she couldn't decide what was right and what was wrong anymore. She was having second thoughts about carrying through with her mother's plan . . . and she hated to admit it, but she had actually started to *like* Ben, and not just for pretend. . . . She found herself wondering if Ben would still be in love with her once the magic ran out. If only she knew what her heart was telling her, she could find the way to who she was meant to be. Right then, she wasn't sure anymore. Was she truly destined for evil?

When Ben had looked into her eyes, had he really seen goodness?

Did she have a choice?

Mal realized Ben had not emerged from the lake. "Ben?" she said, scanning the surface. The water was smooth, with no trace of him. "Ben? *Ben?*" She jumped into the lake and began walking into deeper water, looking for him. But the lake suddenly became too deep, and she thrashed around in a panic.

Ben appeared at her side and carried her back to their picnic area.

Mal sputtered and coughed. "You scared me!" she said, smacking his arm.

"You can't swim?" Ben asked her.

"No!" said Mal.

"You live on an island!" he said.

"Yeah! With a barrier around it, remember?" she said. "Ugh!"

Ben looked at Mal intently. "And you still tried to save me."

She scoffed. "Yeah. And do you thank me? No! All I get is soaking wet!" she said.

"And, uh, this fancy rock," said Ben. He offered her a crystal he'd brought up from the bottom of the lake. "It's yours. Make a wish and throw it back in the lake."

Mal chucked it into the lake, growling, then stood and walked over to sit on the picnic blanket. Ben followed her. He threw his letter jacket over her shoulders and sat next to her.

He touched her wet hair and held her gaze seriously.

"Uh, Mal," he said, "when I told you that I loved you . . . What about you? Do you love me?"

Mal stared long and hard at him, then looked away.

"I don't know what love feels like." Mal sighed.

Ben gently turned her head so she faced him. "Maybe I can teach you," he said.

Mal's heart melted a little. *Maybe he can,* she thought.

CHAPTER FIFTEEN

I'M RETHINKING THIS WHOLE STEALING-THE-WAND THING. DOES BEN ACTUALLY LOVE ME? LIKE, FOR REAL? GAH!

In a classroom, Fairy Godmother strolled up to Mal and her three friends.

"Children," she said, "excuse me, um, as you know, this Sunday is Family Day here at Auradon Prep. And because your parents can't come, due to . . . uh . . . distance . . . we've arranged for a special treat." She walked over to a TV monitor on a cart and clicked a keyboard. A grotesque shot of Maleficent filled the entire screen.

"I don't see anything," said Maleficent, backing up to reveal Evil Queen, Jafar, and Cruella gathered around her. "Nor do I hear . . ." she said.

Fairy Godmother beckoned Mal and her friends to the TV.

They obeyed reluctantly, with Carlos carrying Dude, who was dressed in a jacket.

"Is this thing on?" asked Maleficent. "It's broken!" She clicked away at a remote and threw it down. "I hate electronics."

"Evie!" shouted Evil Queen, watching as an image appeared on their dinky laptop. "It's Mommy!"

Evie waved at the TV monitor.

"Look how beautiful," said Evil Queen. "You know what they say: the poison apple doesn't fall far from the tree."

Cruella cackled.

"Don't you mean the weeds?" said Maleficent.

"Oh! Who's the old *bat*?" asked Cruella, pointing.

"That's Fairy Godmother," said Mal with a smile.

"Still doing tricks with eggplants?" said Maleficent.

"I turned a pumpkin into a beautiful carriage!" said Fairy Godmother.

"You really couldn't give Cinderella till one a.m.?" said Maleficent. "I mean, really. What, the little hamsters had to be back on their little wheels?"

Maleficent, Evil Queen, Jafar, and Cruella laughed.

"They were mice!" said Fairy Godmother. "They were mice."

"Hi, Mom!" said Mal.

"Mal!" Maleficent shouted.

Evil Queen tapped Maleficent's horns, as a reminder to calm down and be discreet.

"M—miss you," said Maleficent.

Jafar said, "You children are never far from our thoughts."

"I got it," Maleficent told Jafar coldly. She turned and spoke to Mal. "How long must Mommy wait to see you? You know Mommy's not good at waiting."

"There's a big coronation coming up," said Mal. "I think probably sometime after that."

Evil Queen's face lit up. "When?" she asked.

"I said I got this!" Maleficent told her. She spoke to Mal. "When?"

"Is there an echo in here?" said Evil Queen.

"Friday! Ten a.m.," said Mal.

"You sure I can't see you before that?" said Maleficent sweetly. "I don't know what I'll do if I don't get my hands on that magic wa—"

Evil Queen tapped Maleficent's horns again.

"You! You little nugget that I love so much!" Maleficent said with a smile.

Jafar, Cruella, and Evil Queen made kissy faces.

"Yes, I completely understand, Mother," said Mal.

Cruella leaned over Maleficent and spoke into the monitor. "Carlos! Is that a *dog*?" She consulted the bejeweled stuffed-animal dog head on her vest. "Yes, yes, Baby, I do understand. It would make the perfect size for earmuffs." She cackled.

"He's the perfect size for a *pet*," said Carlos fiercely, hugging Dude close. "This dog loves me and I love him! And FYI, your dog is stuffed, so give it a rest!"

Cruella stroked Baby. Her lip trembled.

Jafar laughed. "Oh! Burn!" he said.

"Oh, why don't you go sell a toaster, you two-bit salesman?" Cruella told him.

"People who talk to stuffed animals shouldn't throw stones!" said Jafar.

"Oh, well, people who sell toasters shouldn't use mixed metaphors!" said Cruella.

"Enough!" said Evil Queen.

Mal and her friends stood in front of the monitor, shifting their weight and looking at each other, embarrassed. Jay hit the keyboard. The monitor went black.

"I'm so sorry," said Fairy Godmother.

Jay turned to Fairy Godmother. "Thanks for the special treat." He, Mal, Evie, Carlos, and Dude headed out of the classroom, leaving Fairy Godmother behind.

"M," said Evie, "what do you think our parents are going to do to us if we don't pull this off?"

Mal paused. "I think they will be quietly disappointed in us but ultimately proud of us for doing our best," she said with a smile.

"Really?" said Carlos with hope in his voice.

"No, I think we are definitely goners," said Mal, her smile sliding away.

They stomped back to Jay and Carlos's dorm room and began plotting. The group gathered around a table and examined Mal's sketches and a drawn diagram of the cathedral where the coronation would be taking place. Mal had drawn Xs and arrows all over it: a detailed plan of the wand snatch. At the center of the map, Mal had drawn a picture of her hand reaching for the wand that Fairy Godmother held.

"I will be in the very front," said Mal. "You all will be up in the balcony. Carlos?"

"Okay, so I'll find our limo so we can break the barrier and get back on the island with the wand," said Carlos.

Jay looked at him thoughtfully.

"Perfect," said Mal. She lifted a small atomizer, which looked like a pale blue bottle of perfume, and offered it to Evie. "Evie, you will use this to take the driver out," said Mal. She handed the atomizer to Evie. "Two sprays and he will be out like a light."

Mal looked at Carlos, who looked at Jay, who looked at Evie, who looked at Mal. Mal sighed, sat down at the table, and turned to a page in the spell book that read HOW TO BREAK A LOVE SPELL.

Evie peeked at what Mal was reading. "M, you want to break Ben's love spell?" she asked.

"Yeah! You know, for after . . ." said Mal.

Carlos sat on his bed with Dude.

Jay sat on his bed with his tourney stick.

Evie sat down next to Mal.

"I've just been thinking, you know, when the villains finally do invade Auradon and begin to loot and kick everyone out of their castles . . ." said Mal.

Jay spun his tourney stick.

". . . and imprison their leaders . . ." continued Mal.

Carlos absently stroked Dude.

". . . and destroy all that is good and beautiful . . ." Mal said.

Evie took a deep breath and stared off.

". . . Ben still being in love with me just seems a little extra . . . cruel," Mal said.

Evie looked long and hard at her friend.

Mal closed her spell book and headed back to their dorm room.

Evie followed shortly after.

Jay flicked off all the lights and climbed into bed. Then he got up and walked over to his tourney trophy.

Carlos patted Dude.

In the girls' dorm room, Evie lay in bed awake. She pulled the chemistry test out from under her pillow and reveled in the B+ again. The other bed was empty.

Mal was in the kitchen stirring a potion. The spell book was open. Alone and lonely, Mal finally allowed herself to feel . . . and her heart was breaking. She knew it wasn't right for Ben to be under her love spell. She felt guilty and horrible about it.

Enchanting him was a rotten thing to do—one she couldn't bear any longer. Ben was good and kind and deserved to be spell-free—even if it meant he no longer loved her. A tear rolled down her face and dropped into the chocolate batter. Next to the bowl was a beautiful little blue box. She'd break the love spell right before the coronation. As for stealing the wand, she wasn't so sure she'd be able to walk away from that one.

CHAPTER SIXTEEN

F AMILY DAY.
OH, JOY.

The next morning, the sun shone over the rose garden on a breezy Family Day.

On the green lawn, Ben led a choir of students in singing "Be Our Guest" as a way to kick off the event. A student banner read FAMILY DAY! GOODNESS DOESN'T GET ANY BETTER. Some students and their families danced, while others enjoyed plates of every type of delicious food imaginable from various tables and tents.

Mal grabbed a strawberry from a table as she, Evie, Jay, and Carlos stepped into the throng. Carlos handed off Dude to Evie and ate strawberries he dipped in a lavishly flowing chocolate fountain.

The happy choir dispersed. Mal nibbled her strawberry and watched Ben join Beast and Belle. They stepped under a stone archway and posed for the photographer.

"Oh! And by the way, I have a new girlfriend," Ben told his parents.

They looked at him and gasped.

"I never wanted to say anything," said Belle, "but I always thought that Audrey was a little self-absorbed. With a fake smile"—Belle flashed a fake smile for the photographer and continued to speak through it—"a kind of kiss-up."

"Do we know your new girlfriend?" asked Beast.

"On the count of three," said the photographer. "One . . . two . . ."

"Sort of . . ." Ben said, waving at Mal, who waved back. "Mal!" he called to her.

"Three!" said the photographer.

Belle's and Beast's frozen looks of shock were captured in the photo.

"Mal! Mal, I want to introduce you to my parents," he said, going over to her. They hugged. He turned to his parents. "This is Mal. From the island. My girlfriend."

"Hi," said Belle, gawking.

"Hi," said Mal.

Beast waved.

"I was thinking maybe she could join us for lunch," said Ben.

"Of course," Beast said. "Any friend of Ben's—"

"Um, I actually came with my friends," said Mal.

"Well," said Belle, "you should . . . invite them."

Belle gazed past Mal at the girl's three friends. Jay was drinking directly from the chocolate fountain as Carlos, his face smeared with chocolate, jumped up and down, giggling, and dipped more strawberries into the fountain. Evie bounced Dude up and down in her arms.

Belle smiled kindly. "The more, the merrier!"

"Okay!" said Mal, smiling. "I'll go grab them." She turned to get her friends.

"How about a game of croquet before lunch?" asked Beast.

"Of course!" said Mal.

"Game on!" said Ben, high-fiving his dad.

"Game on," said Beast. He laughed. Belle smiled.

As Mal and Ben walked toward the croquet lawn, Belle's and Beast's smiles vanished. Belle nearly fainted, and Beast caught her.

Mal happily trotted toward her friends. *Maybe we will have a nice time after all,* she thought. She walked onto the lawn, picked up a croquet stick, and hit the ball. Students frolicked around her. Mal smiled at an older woman in a pale pink suit, Queen Leah.

"Hello there," said Queen Leah, strolling up to her with a smile.

"Hi," said Mal.

"Now, have we met?" asked Queen Leah.

"No, I don't think so," said Mal. "I'm new. I'm sort of like a transfer student."

Audrey appeared beside them in a pink dress, holding a glass of punch.

"Grammy!" Audrey said.

"Oh, Audrey!" said the woman. "Give Grammy a kiss, dear."

"*'Grammy'?*" said Mal.

"Sleeping Beauty's mother," said Audrey. She turned to her grandmother. "Grammy, I don't think you want to be talking to this girl. Unless you feel like taking another hundred-year nap." Audrey shot Mal a nasty smile.

Queen Leah stared hard at Mal. "What?" She backed away from Mal in horror, mistaking her for Maleficent. *"You!"* she cried. "How are you here? And how have you stayed so young?"

Everybody in the garden grew quiet and gathered around them.

Ben rushed over to them. "Queen Leah, it's okay," he said. "Maleficent is still on the island. This is her daughter, Mal." He put a hand on Mal's arm. "Don't you remember my proclamation to give the new generation a chance?" He smiled at her.

"A chance to *what*, Ben?" said Queen Leah. *"Destroy* us?" She looked around at all the adults. "You remember, don't you?" she said, turning to her audience. "The poison apples. And the spells!" Beast, Belle, Fairy Godmother, and the others all stared at her solemnly. "The spells . . . My daughter was raised by fairies because of your mother's curse. Her first words, her first steps—I missed it *all*!" Queen Leah turned away, sobbing quietly. Mal went to comfort her.

"I'm so sorry—" said Mal.

Chad jumped between them. "Go away! Step away from her!" Chad told Mal.

"Don't do this, Chad," said Ben.

"What? They were raised by their *parents*, Ben," said Chad. "What do you think villains teach their children? Kindness? Fair play? No way, okay?"

The other students looked at Mal and her friends with growing suspicion.

Chad turned to face Mal. "You stole another girl's boyfriend." He pointed at Jay. "You enjoy hurting people." He spun on Evie. "And you! You're nothing but a gold digger and a cheater!" He smiled and looked at the audience.

Evie yanked out her mirror. "Mirror, mirror, in my hand, who's the biggest jerk in the land?" She held the mirror up to Chad.

"What? Come on!" said Chad, slapping the mirror away.

Jay grabbed Chad. "Hey! Watch it!" said Jay.

They started to tussle. Evie leaped in and squirted Chad with the atomizer. He fell to the ground immediately. The garden broke into pandemonium. Mal and her three friends ran out of the garden.

"Guys!" Ben called after them. He looked around at the chaos. His plan was falling to pieces. Chad finally came to.

"I feared something like this would happen," said Beast.

"This isn't their fault!" said Ben.

"No, Son," said Beast solemnly, "it's yours." He and Belle walked away from their son.

Ben straightened to bear the full weight of the disaster.

Ben took off after Mal and her friends. When lunch rolled around, he finally found them outside at a picnic table. None of them spoke. A ring of empty tables surrounded them, and beyond that sat the others in their cliques, staring them down.

"Hey, guys! How is everyone?" asked Ben.

They didn't respond.

"Hey, listen, forget about today," he said. "It was

nothing. Forget about it. Let it go." He rested his hands on Mal's shoulders.

Mal kept staring straight ahead, not acknowledging him.

"Tomorrow after the coronation, I promise everything will be okay," said Ben.

Mal and her three friends looked glum.

"I have to go," Ben said. "I'll see you guys later." He walked away.

Doug strolled up to the table. "Hey, listen, Evie, I want to talk—"

"Doug!" shouted Chad from another table.

"It's my fault. I'm so sorry—" Evie whispered to Doug.

"Doug!" Chad barked again.

"Doug . . ." Evie said.

"I'm sorry, I can't," said Doug. He joined Chad at his table.

Evie pushed her food tray away huffily.

Audrey strolled past with Jane. Audrey talked loudly enough for Mal and her friends to hear. "How long does she think that's going to last? She's just the bad-girl infatuation." Audrey shot them a cruel smile.

"Yeah," said Jane. "I mean, he's never going to make a villain a queen."

Most of the girls laughed, and Audrey and Jane walked off.

Mal glowered and flipped through her spell book, waving her finger. *"Beware, forswear, undo Jane's hair."*

Jane screamed as her short bob replaced the long wavy brown locks. Jane's friends backed away, pointing and laughing at her hairdo. Jane looked mortified.

Lonnie stroked her own hair, making sure it was still long and glamorous.

"There's a lot more where that came from," Mal told the girls.

"Excuse me, who do you think you are?" asked Audrey, hand on her hip.

"Do I look like I'm kidding?" Mal asked.

When the girls kept on staring at her, she opened her spell book again.

The girls and their friends took off.

Mal was angry. She spun around to her friends. "I'm really looking forward to tomorrow," she said, slamming her book shut. "Let's grab that wand and blow this Popsicle stand."

Evie, Jay, and Carlos looked at Mal and nodded in quiet understanding. They got up from the picnic table and walked fiercely back toward the school in their usual Isle of the Lost gang formation. Their focus was back. It was nearly coronation time— their big moment to steal the wand. The four were rotten to the core after all.

CHAPTER SEVENTEEN

O PERATION WAND-JACKING IS OFFICIALLY A GO. THEY WANT EVIL? WE'LL SHOW THESE SUCKERS EVIL.

AURADON PREP KIDS WILL GET WHAT'S COMING TO THEM. MALEFICENT'S DAUGHTER IS BACK.

Ben's coronation at the cathedral was a grand event like no other.

The cloudless blue sky smiled down upon limos snaking their way up to the entrance of the cathedral. The cathedral steps were lined with a royal-blue carpet, brimming with honored guests. Blue and gold flags rustled in the fair breeze. Snow White, the anchorwoman, stood on a platform facing a TV cameraman.

"At last!" Snow White said into her mike. "Here

we are, broadcasting live from the coronation, where Prince Benjamin will soon be crowned king! I'm Snow White, bringing you up-to-the-second coverage of who's the fairest of them all!"

The camera exposed the inside of the massive cathedral, with its stained glass and countless pillars. It panned over Audrey, Chad, Jane, Fairy Godmother, and other guests mingling beside a stage, where a bell jar was on display, covered by a sheet.

"Aw, Fairy Godmother is looking radiant," said Snow White. "But what is happening with Jane's hair! And that Peter Pan collar with a pink bow? Someone just earned a spot on Snow White's 'That Don't Look Right' list!" She waved a hand.

Fairy Godmother uncovered the bell jar to reveal her magic wand.

"And there's Fairy Godmother's wand!" said Snow White. "So sparkly! So fun!

"Oh! And here comes Ben now!" Snow White announced.

A carriage drawn by two white horses rolled up in front of the cathedral. Ben and Mal sat in the back. Mal wore a radiant purple dress and had her hair up in a fancy bun. Ben wore his deep blue suit. Guests threw flower petals and confetti at them.

"Ooh, and he went with classic prince couture. *That* is a Benja-*win*," said Snow White.

Inside the carriage, Mal clutched her blue box. She looked down at it.

Ben took her hand. "Don't be nervous," he told her. "All you have to do is sit there and look beautiful." He smiled. "No problem there."

"Thank you," said Mal. She looked back at the box in her lap.

Ben offered his Auradon Prep ring to her. "Mal, would you wear my ring?"

"Um! Not now," she said, pulling her hand out of his. "I think it would just fall right off me." She smiled. "I have something for you!" She handed him the beautiful blue box. "It's just for later. You know, when you need strength . . . some carbs to keep up your energy."

"Always thinking," said Ben, opening the box. Inside was a chocolate mini cupcake. "But I can't wait." He took a big bite of the treat.

"No!" said Mal, reaching to stop him.

Ben munched the cupcake. "Mmm, this is really good."

Mal looked apprehensively at him. "Uh . . . do you feel okay?"

"You bet!" said Ben, licking his fingers.

"Would you say that you're still in lo—that you have very strong feelings for me?" asked Mal.

"Not sure," said Ben. "Let's give the anti-love potion a few minutes to take effect."

"Okay," said Mal. Then she realized what he'd said. She stared at him.

He laughed.

She laughed, too. "You knew?" she asked.

"What? That you spelled me? Yeah," said Ben. "Yeah, I knew."

"I can explain myself—" started Mal.

"It's fine. You had a crush on me. I was with Audrey. You just didn't trust that it could happen on its own," said Ben. "Am I right?"

"Exactly. You are so right," said Mal. "So then, how long have you known?"

"Since our first date," said Ben. "Your spell washed away in the Enchanted Lake."

"So then . . . what, you've just been faking it since then?" asked Mal.

Ben put his ring on Mal's finger and kissed her hand.

"I haven't been faking anything," Ben said, looking deep into her eyes.

The carriage rolled to a stop in front of the cathedral. Trumpets blared. Footmen opened the carriage door and helped Mal down from it.

"Well, if it isn't Mal looking like some kind of princess!" said Snow White. "Now, let's see who this beauty is wearing. . . ." Snow White read something from a blue index card. "Evie!" she said. "Someone named *Evie* designed her gown."

Ben took her hand. He and Mal walked up the cathedral stairs. Trumpets blared on either side of them as they approached Beast and Belle. The crowd roared.

Mal and Ben reached the top of the stairs. Mal bowed before Ben's parents.

"About the other day, I just—" Mal said to Beast.

"I told Ben this wasn't going to be easy," said Beast.

"You also taught me that a king has to believe in himself," said Ben. "Even when it isn't easy."

"I did? How very wise of me," said Beast.

Belle took Ben's hands in hers. "Ben, we are very proud of you," said Belle. "You keep listening to your heart."

"Thanks, Mom," said Ben.

"You're going to make a fine king," said Beast. He patted Ben on the arm.

Beast and Belle walked off. Ben stepped up to Mal. "Wish me luck."

An attendant offered his hand to Mal. She turned to Ben, smiled, and allowed herself to be led away and into the cathedral. It was time to begin the coronation.

Attendants opened the main doors to the cathedral for Ben. He began to walk down the long aisle. The audience bowed to him as he passed. A choir sang. Mal watched Ben from the front row. Evie, Jay, and Carlos with Dude looked on from the balcony. Ben moved down the aisle. Mal smiled. But her smile fell.

Ben approached the stage where Fairy God-mother, his parents, and the wand waited for him. Mal was so very close to the wand. In her mind, she could picture her mother and the other villains cheering at the sight of her so close to it, watching her with burning intensity. Mal could almost hear her mother say under her breath, "Don't blow this, kiddo." She gulped and stared at Ben as Fairy Godmother lifted the crown from Beast's head and placed it on Ben's as he kneeled. Mal had never before seen him look so noble. Her stomach lurched as she stared intently at the wand.

Mal's eyes began to glass over with tears.

Beast lifted the bell jar.

Belle handed the wand to Fairy Godmother.

Mal looked at Evie, who nodded and gave Carlos and Jay the signal to proceed with their plan. Then she looked back at the wand. It shimmered. Mal stared at it, transfixed. Before the Fairy Godmother, Ben awaited the blessing with her wand.

The choir stopped singing.

Fairy Godmother held the wand out to Ben as

if she were going to knight him. "Do you solemnly swear to govern the peoples of Auradon," said Fairy Godmother for all in the cathedral to hear, "with justice and mercy as long as you shall reign?"

Mal could just picture her mother shouting for her to grab the wand.

"I do solemnly swear," said Ben.

Fairy Godmother lifted the wand. "Then it is my honor and my joy to bless our new king—"

The wand was snatched out of Fairy Godmother's hand.

The audience gasped.

CHAPTER EIGHTEEN

T HE MOMENT OF TRUTH HAS ARRIVED.
WHY DO I FEEL SO UNPREPARED?

The magic wand shook violently and shot off a wild display of sparks.

It bucked and sent a fierce bolt of lightning that cracked through one of the cathedral's stained glass windows. The bolt sizzled through the air and exploded as it hit and broke the magic barrier of the Isle of the Lost. Maleficent's house rumbled.

Fairy Godmother was wide-eyed. "Child, what are you doing?" she cried.

But it wasn't Mal who brandished the wand; it was *Jane*!

Jane shouted, "If you won't make me beautiful,

I'll do it myself!" She struggled to control the wand as its power rocked her viciously from side to side.

Everyone screamed as the wand swung left and then right.

"Bibbidi-Bobbidi-Boo!" said Jane.

She spun frantically as the room watched in horror.

"Take cover!" Beast shouted to the terrified audience.

Beast shielded Belle, and Ben put an arm over Mal.

The audience leaped back from the shower of sparks.

Mal ran up to Jane and pried the wand from her hands.

"Careful, Mal!" said Belle.

Mal wielded the wand like a sword. The audience ducked. Mal looked at her friends in the balcony, and they ran downstairs and raced toward her.

Jane scampered away from her.

Ben moved toward Mal. "Mal . . . give me the wand," he said.

"Stand back," said Mal.

"Mal, it's okay—" started Ben.

"Ben, I said *stand back*!" said Mal, brandishing the wand fiercely.

Audrey stepped out from the fray. "I told you so!" she said to Ben.

Mal swung the wand toward her, and Audrey staggered backward.

The audience gasped and screamed, then fell quiet.

Evie, Jay, and Carlos stepped behind Mal.

"Let's go!" said Carlos.

"Revenge time," said Jay.

"You really want to do this?" Ben asked Mal.

"We don't have a choice, Ben!" said Mal. "Our parents—"

"Your parents made their choices," said Ben. "Now you make yours."

Mal looked into the faces of Beast, Belle, and Fairy Godmother. Then she took a moment to think about it.

"I think I want to be good," said Mal.

"You *are* good," said Ben.

"How do you know that?" said Mal.

"Because . . . because I'm listening to my heart," Ben said.

Mal lowered the wand ever so slightly. "I want to listen to my heart, too," she said. "And my heart is telling me that we are *not* our parents." Mal lowered the wand more and faced her friends. She looked at Jay. "I mean, stealing things doesn't make you happy. Tourney and victory pizza with the team makes you happy."

Jay smiled.

She looked at Carlos. "And you, scratching Dude's belly makes you happy. Who would've thought?" She giggled. She looked at Evie. "And, Evie, you do not have to play dumb to get a guy. You are so smart."

Evie laughed, nodding, and shed happy tears.

Mal said, "And I don't want to take over the world with evil. I want to go to school. And be with Ben." She turned to look at him. "Because Ben makes me really happy." She held up her hand with his ring on her finger and smiled. She turned back to her friends. "Us being friends makes me really happy. Not destroying things. . . ."

Evie, Jay, and Carlos nodded at her.

"I choose good, you guys." She put her hand out.

"I choose good, too," said Jay, joining her fist with his.

Evie put her fist next to Jay's. "I choose good," she said, smiling.

Carlos took a deep breath. "So, just to be clear: we don't have to be worried about how really mad our parents will be? Because they're gonna be really, really mad."

Mal, Evie, and Jay laughed.

"Your parents can't reach you here," said Ben.

"Okay, then . . . Good." Carlos smiled and added his fist to the circle.

Mal laughed and nodded at Ben, beckoning him over to them.

Ben put his hand in the mix, too. Mal leaned against him and smiled.

Then the sound of a window shattering caused

everyone to gasp. A green glowing orb floated down from the broken window and landed beside Mal and her friends.

In a flash of lightning and a roll of thunder, Maleficent appeared.

CHAPTER NINETEEN

Of course. Mom always has to ruin *everything*.

The audience froze as Maleficent threw back her head.

"I'm baaaaaaaaack!" Maleficent said.

"Go away, Mother," said Mal.

Maleficent chuckled. "You're very funny," she said. In one hand, she held her scepter. She extended her other hand. "Here—wand me," she said. When Mal didn't move, she snapped her fingers. "Chop-chop!"

Mal made as if to give the wand to Maleficent.

"No!" said Ben.

Instead, Mal threw the wand to Fairy Godmother, who caught it.

"Bibbidi-Bobbidi—" started Fairy Godmother.

"*Boo!*" said Maleficent. With a fearsome wave of her scepter, she froze everyone except for Mal, Evie, Carlos, and Jay. "Psych!" Maleficent chuckled darkly.

Maleficent took her time crossing over to Beast. She took off his glasses and put them back on his head. She hummed an evil ditty and walked over to Fairy Godmother. She plucked the wand from Fairy Godmother's hand. The wand sparked in protest. "Where shall we begin?" she said. She pointed the wand at Mal. "I know. Why don't we start by getting rid of this. . . ." She aimed the wand at Ben's ring on Mal's finger. The ring flew into Maleficent's hand. "Perfect fit!" She walked over to Ben and knocked his crown askance. "Falling in love is weak . . . and *ridiculous*," she said. She looked at her daughter. "It's not what you want."

"You don't know what I want!" said Mal. "Mom, have you ever once asked *me* what I want?" Tears streamed down Mal's cheeks. "I'm not you!" she said.

"Well, obviously!" said Maleficent. "I've had years and years and years and years of practice being evil. You'll get there."

"No, I will not!" said Mal. "And I really wish that you had never gotten there yourself." She looked at her mom and felt sorry for her. "Love is not weak or ridiculous. It's actually really amazing." She smiled through her tears.

"I know one thing, young lady. You have *no room* for love in your life!" said Maleficent. She pointed the wand at Mal.

Mal extended her hand. *"And now I command, wand to my hand!"* she yelled. The wand flew into her hand. "It worked!" Mal said.

Mal, Evie, Jay, and Carlos exchanged looks.

"I hardly think so," Maleficent told Mal. "Frankly, this is tedious and very immature. Give me the wand! Give me the wand!"

"Hold on, Mal!" said Carlos. "Maybe good really is more powerful than evil."

Maleficent laughed. "Oh, please. You're killing me!" She barked like a dog.

Dude ran up and jumped into her arms.

"Off! Off! Breath! The breath! Get off me!" She threw Dude off her.

Jay, seizing the moment, dove in to grab the scepter.

Maleficent held it tightly. She leaned in close to him and stroked his bicep. "Gaston should be jealous," she said. With a flick, she sent Jay flying backward.

Maleficent cackled, then faced Mal and her friends. "Enough!" she boomed. "You all will regret this!" She began to expand and change shape into a huge dragon. Maleficent the dragon soared above them. They gasped as she roared and swiveled her scaly head, getting Jay in her sights. She hovered, ready to strike.

"Jay!" cried Mal.

He ran down the aisle. The dragon flew and followed him.

"She's right behind you!" shouted Carlos.

"Jay!" shouted Mal.

Jay sprinted away from the dragon.

"Jay, run!" called Evie.

Mal watched in horror as the dragon flew the length of the aisle, overtaking Jay quickly. As Maleficent swooped down on him, talons gleaming, Evie stepped between them and reflected a beam of sunlight with her mirror. It blinded the dragon, who came skidding to a sudden stop.

Mal leaped between them and her mother, holding out the wand. "Leave my friends alone!" she said. "This is between you and me, Mother!"

The dragon slowly bent her head down until it was level with Mal. Mal was dwarfed by the monster. The dragon cackled—an echoing reminder that Maleficent was still in there. The dragon met Mal's eyes, assured of victory.

Mal didn't blink. Her eyes flashed green. In the reflection of the dragon's eyes, Mal stood fearless, beautiful, and strong. She incanted confidently, *"The strength of evil is good as none, when stands before four hearts as one."* Mal said it again, louder: *"The strength of evil is good as none, when stands before four hearts as one."* Mal repeated the words a final time, with even more force: *"The strength of evil is good as none, when stands before four hearts as one!"* Before, Mal had always lost the stare-downs she'd had with her mother. But in that moment, the dragon blinked.

There was a flash of smoke, and the dragon was gone.

Mal gasped. She, Evie, Jay, and Carlos looked at one another and smiled.

"What just happened?" asked Carlos.

"I have no idea," said Mal, racing down the aisle.

Her friends followed her.

"Did you do it?" asked Evie.

"I don't know!" said Mal, stopping short.

Fairy Godmother unfroze and ran to meet them in the aisle.

"No, no, no," said Fairy Godmother, who stood looking at them with warmth and pride. "Your mother did," she said gently to Mal. "She shrank to the size of the love in her heart. That's why it's so . . . itty-bitty." She looked down at their feet.

Where there had once been a dragon, there now was a tiny lizard.

Mal asked, "Is she going to be like that forever?"

"Forever is a long time," said Fairy Godmother warmly. "You learned how to love. So can she."

Mal smiled. She held the wand out to Fairy Godmother. "I believe this belongs to you."

Fairy Godmother took the wand and picked up Ben's ring from the ground. "And I believe *this* belongs to you." She held it out to Mal.

Mal grinned and put on the ring.

Fairy Godmother looked at Mal's friends. "You all have earned yourselves an A in Goodness class."

Mal and her friends laughed. Evie gave Mal a high five.

Fairy Godmother aimed her wand at Ben, Beast, and Belle. "Bibbidi-Bobbidi-Boo!" she said.

Ben roared a battle cry.

Mal stopped him. "Okay, okay, okay! We kind of all got this wrapped up here," she said.

Fairy Godmother unfroze the other Auradonians.

Ben looked around, confused, and then swept Mal into a hug.

Mal squealed.

"Next time, I rescue you, okay?" he said.

"Yeah. Let's not have there be a next time, okay?"

said Mal. She gave him a hug, then straightened his crown on his head. She giggled and said, "I will be right back."

Mal walked over to Fairy Godmother, who was lecturing Jane.

"I love you, but you are on a major time-out," said Fairy Godmother, pointing the wand at Jane.

"Don't be too hard on Jane," Mal said, putting a hand on Fairy Godmother's shoulder. "I was the one who put all that crazy stuff in her head." She locked eyes with a humiliated Jane. "*You* are beautiful, inside and out. Your mom got that right."

"I guess I did get pretty lucky in the mother department," Jane said.

Mal smiled. "Yeah! I guess so," she said.

Fairy Godmother took Jane's hand and led her away.

Mal locked eyes with Audrey. Mal smiled and curtsied. Audrey did the same. Their not getting along was water under the bridge, for real that time.

An attendant clamped the bell jar over the lizard in the aisle.

Mal leaped toward them. "Hey! Careful!" she said. "That's my mom!"

The audience laughed, and the attendant bowed and walked away.

Mal, Ben, Evie, Jay, and Carlos with Dude huddled together.

"Let's get this party started!" said Jay.

The friends all whooped and cheered. They were ready for the coronation celebration.

CHAPTER TWENTY

THIS "HAPPILY EVER AFTER" THING ISN'T AS LAME AS IT SOUNDS.

WE PARTIED INTO THE NIGHT.

That evening, outside the school, the whole student body set it off and partied.

Ben twirled Mal. Evie danced fiercely with Doug. Jay and Carlos danced with Jane. Then Jay danced with Audrey. Fireworks exploded in the sky above the school. Chad jived. Lonnie boogied. It was a hip-hop fairy-tale rave.

The lights flashed. The music blasted.

Mal looked into Ben's eyes. The sky was lit up with sparklers behind him. She touched her nose to his. In that moment, Mal couldn't help smiling. She never would have thought, in her wildest dreams, that her story would have a happy ending.